What She Saw

Sara McFerrin

A Trunk Doctor Mystery

This is a work of fiction. Names, characters, places, and events that occur are either the products of the author's imagination or are used fictitiously. Any resemblance to actual persons, places, or events is purely coincidental.

ISBN 10: 0-9994785-4-0
ISBN 13: 978-0-9994785-4-7

Cover Design: Charlotte Rose Mermoud

Contact the author at: www.saramcferrin.com or saramcferrin@mediacombb.net

Dedication

To Gayle Kriegel

Acknowledgements

It takes a village is an African proverb meaning that it takes an entire community to raise a child. The same principal applies to producing a book.

A very special thanks to the following villagers: Tom Gray, Barbara Klyce, Pete Howard, Beverly LeBoeuf, Geni Mermoud, Charlotte Mermoud, Melisa Taylor, Jake Keeling, and a slew of family, friends, and followers whose encouragement and support propelled me to the end.

Books by Sara McFerrin

Curiosity Club Mystery Series:

Southern Ladies' Curiosity Club
Whatever Happened to Mildred?
Sunken Secrets
The Ghost of Stupid Mistakes

Southern Quickies:

Conversations: Beebe's Facelift
Conversations: Marian's Last Wish
Conversations: In Good Hands

Other Titles:

Whistlin' Stardust

Raney Days: David G. Raney Family &
Their Antebellum Home

Chapter One

"There's something in there. It's heavy an' it rattles." Ernest Lawson tried another key. So far, none had fit the latch, and he was running out of keys to try.

Jix Haynes knelt on the shop floor beside the locksmith. Christened with her mother's maiden name of Jixson, she'd spent a lifetime repeating, spelling, and explaining her unusual name. Although a scourge during her adolescent years when she'd desperately wanted to be a Susan or a Sandra, she'd grown into a strong, opinionated, undeniable Jix. The name suited her to a tee.

A perpetual optimist, the perky, dishwater blonde was confident Ernest would not rest until he'd opened the battered old trunk.

She chatted as he jimmied the keyless hasp, "The owner says it's been locked for thirty years, at least. Recently, she inherited the trunk from her aunt. The story goes they knew there was a key and kept thinking they'd run across it, so they never broke into the trunk. And they never found the key."

"Well, I'll get it open. Ain't no such gonna outfox Ole Ernie!" A third generation locksmith, Ernest prided himself on being a wizard when it came to locking mechanisms.

Jix chuckled. Every trunk she'd brought to the Lawson Locksmith and Bicycle Repair Shop had been successfully opened, and only once had Ernest had to break the fastener.

Fortunately, most trunks were unlatched when they were entrusted to the Trunk Doctor to be restored to their former glory. Forty-six damaged or decomposing trunks were stacked against the back wall in the Haynes' garage waiting for a facelift: camel backs, travel trunks, trunks covered in canvas, leather, or tin.

Once he had abandoned hope of finding a skeleton key, Ernest tried a lock pick.

"There it goes!" he shouted.

Jix clapped her hands as Ernest lifted the lid, providing an escape route for that peculiar, musty odor items acquire when stored for a long time. They peered inside.

"I don't know what we expected, but we didn't find gold coins or bundles of hundred dollar bills." Their high hopes dissipated with the musty odor. Jix admired a pair of black, high button shoes lying side-by-side in the open section of the tray. "How tiny these are! People were smaller when these were in style."

With one finger, Ernest lifted the convex lid to the glove box located on the right-hand side of the tray. Inside the unintended time capsule, they found gloves, tintypes, a string of pearls, cameo broaches, a button hook, a tress of ginger-colored hair tied with thin blue ribbon and wrapped in tissue paper, among other odds and ends.

A quick glance through layers of neatly stacked books and papers produced nothing worthy of immediate attention although Jix's curiosity was aroused when Ernest pulled a diary from underneath a stack of yellowed sheet music.

Jix grabbed a rope handle that had been rigged to replace a missing leather handle. Ernest clutched the other, and they loaded the trunk onto Jix's short-bed pickup truck. Bright red and blue letters painted on white doors advertised The Trunk Doctor's services and phone number.

A cautious driver, the fifty-two-year-old grandmother glanced in the side and rear view mirrors before pulling into traffic. A black sedan leaving a parking spot waited for Jix to go first. She assumed this was a courteous gesture since the car was a block away and on the opposite side of the street with ample time to go ahead.

The dashboard clock read nearly noon. She needed to go home and check on her mother who lived with Jix and Jix's husband Bill. She would unload the trunk and then warm leftovers for lunch.

The Haynes' daughter, Carol, and her fifteen-month-old toddler, Dinah, also lived with the family while Carol's husband, Scotty, was temporarily out of the country. A once-in-a-lifetime opportunity to participate in a program to teach English in Thailand and China had come his way, and Carol had insisted he go. She could have gone too, but that would have required she give up a good-paying job she loved, so when her mother offered her room and board for the eight-month term of the teaching tour, she moved back home. Jix and her mother helped with Dinah; Carol took over childcare duties on her days off.

Without serious consideration, intentions to go straight home took an unplanned detour when Jix hung a quick right at an intersection and drove away from her neighborhood.

She wouldn't stay long. Although it was lunchtime, and she had not called ahead, Jix knew Abby Gayle Kamp, her friend and antiquing buddy, would extend a warm welcome and be excited to explore the contents of the trunk.

Jix's eyes shifted to the rear view mirror as she flipped on the left blinker and braked to turn into the Kamp's driveway. The only other vehicle on the residential street was a black car that appeared to be keeping its distance. Jix parked behind Abby Gayle's SUV, turned off the ignition, and waited for the sedan to pass. After a moderate wait, the leery, trunk restorer got out, walked to the end of the driveway, and looked in both directions. The car was not in sight.

Abby Gayle was watering flowers in the side yard. When she'd seen her friend turn into the driveway, she'd put the garden hose aside and walked over to the truck. Welcoming an opportunity to look in a vintage chest, she insisted Jix bring the trunk inside. They lugged the heavy thing through the garage and into the den.

"Put it here." They lowered it to the floor. Abby Gayle slid two hassocks side-by-side, and then with a hefty jerk they landed it atop the footstools.

"Sorry, I didn't call. Are you busy? I remembered Austin is on a long haul. Ernest opened Paula Manikin's trunk, and I thought we might see what's inside. Hope I'm not intruding." Jix gave her friend a hug.

"Don't be silly. I'm always glad to see you. Austin called from Cincinnati last night. He'll be home on Tuesday. Wednesday is our fifteenth wedding anniversary...it's been a long haul," she quipped. "Have you had lunch? I made tomato-basil soup with tomatoes from the garden, and I'll grill us a cheese sandwich."

"Oh, Abby Gayle, that sounds wonderful. I don't have much time; I need to get home and check on things there."

"Call while I get the sandwiches ready and tell them where you are. You want pickle on your grilled cheese?" The spunky, raven-haired, young woman called over her shoulder on her way to the kitchen.

"No, thank you. Do you have strawberry or grape jelly?"

"Strawberry. Why?"

Jix hesitated. "I'll spread a little on my sandwich."

"Why am I not surprised? This comes from a person who puts potato chips on peanut butter sandwiches," she laughed.

"Don't knock it 'til you've tried it."

A phone call confirmed the family's whereabouts. Her mother, Margee, had eaten lunch and was about to take a nap, Carol and Dinah were on their way home to also take a nap, and Bill had called to say he would be out of his office at Mid-State Mortgage all afternoon but hoped to be home by five-thirty or six.

The Trunk Doctor's only employee, a gentle-soul in his late forties named Earl Jones had run into a problem on a trunk and needed to talk to Jix. Once she'd gotten Earl back on track, the ladies enjoyed a hot bowl of soup and a sandwich.

Abby Gayle suggested she set up a card table near the trunk so they could sort items and keep them within reach. She always brought order when she and Jix did anything together. This was a good thing because Jix Haynes was not intimidated by clutter or lack of organization; she preferred the familiarity of both. The two women complimented each other. Were it not for Jix, Abby Gayle would have organized her life into a *mise en place* prison, stifling every spark of spontaneity. On the other hand, Abby Gayle's knack for order had more than once prevented otherwise problematic circumstances for Jix. Each relied upon the other's strengths.

Once the dishes were loaded and the food put away, the curiosity driven duo dove into the old trunk's trove of trinkets that concealed secrets of long-gone lives.

Chapter Two

"I assume you will return these things to your client," Abby Gayle stood over the table of neatly sorted items. She checked each against a list she'd compiled in a spiral notebook. Included in the list was a key found in the glove box portion of the tray. Jix had inserted the tiny key in the diary's clasp, and with a click, the strap holding the book closed sprang loose.

Sitting cross-legged on the carpet, Jix replied, "I'll box everything and give it to Paula. The oldest of her five daughters graduated from high school, and Paula's husband surprised his wife and kids with a holiday in Tuscany. This trunk is for the graduate. I have a month to restore it...plenty of time."

Abby Gayle turned the photographs over hoping to find information written on the back. "I think the woman deserves a trip, although I would have wanted to go alone or with a friend, not with five daughters."

"To each his own," Jix said as she fingered the worn, beige cover of the book she held in her lap. Whether an attempt to personalize the cover or decorate it, the owner—presumably—had doodled an inked border of hearts and flowers, birds in flight, and x's and o's. A large heart encircled the initials B. A. P. and R. V. Q.

"The diary belonged to…" she opened to the first page, "…someone named Bethany Ann Perkins who, judging by the artwork, was clearly a dreamer and a doodler. I feel badly about invading her privacy. I doubt she intended for anyone else to read this."

"I won't tell, and she'll never know," Abby Gayle casually commented and turned her attention to the stacks of photographs. "Several of these photos have names written on the back. Judging by the clothes, I'd say most were taken in the late forties, maybe the fifties." She reached for a stack of tintypes and added, "These are older…probably dating back to the eighteen eighties."

"Anybody named Perkins?"

Sorting through the stack of glossy, black-and-white snapshots, Abby Gayle selected one. "This one is labeled Bethany. Could be the same. It's a girl sitting on the hood of a car. Whoever took the shot must have wanted a photo of the car as well. Nineteen fifty-six Chevy. Sharp ride! Austin has always wanted one." She handed the photo to Jix.

"She's too far away to see her facial features clearly. If they hadn't included the car in the frame, we would have had a close-up of her," Abby Gayle pointed out the obvious.

Jix looked closely at the girl in her late teens with dark hair resting on her shoulders. The young lady wore a plaid, circular skirt, black-and-white saddle oxfords, and a varsity high school jacket draped over her shoulders. "Could be the same Bethany," she repeated.

Jix hurriedly thumbed through to the final journal entry and focused on the date scrawled in green ink. "Her last post was on Friday, June seventh, nineteen hundred and fifty-seven." She thumbed through the remaining blank pages. "Why did she stop writing?"

"She was tired of writing in a diary. She moved away and left the diary behind. She took a trip for the rest of the summer; she eloped with someone and started a new diary. She…."

"Okay, I get it. There could be a dozen reasons why she didn't continue." Jix stuck the photo between pages, unfolded her legs, stood, and placed the diary on the table. "I'll read this tonight to satisfy my curiosity. I have to go; I have lots to do before Bill gets home. Let's get these things boxed. No need to put it back in the trunk and have to sort it again. I have a box in the truck."

"There are boxes in the garage. I think we can get everything into one."

The ladies arranged all but the diary in a cardboard box, taped it shut, and labeled it P. Manikin. "You are welcome to leave it here. That will be one less thing to keep up with, and you can pick the box up when you're ready to deliver the trunk."

Jix welcomed the suggestion, tossed the diary and key into the tray of the empty trunk, and helped move the box to the garage. Once Paula Manikin's trunk was bungeed securely in the truck, Jix headed for home.

When she arrived, Earl was there to unload. He intended to place the trunk with the others, as trunks were usually dealt with in order of arrival, but Jix, remembering to retrieve the diary, told Earl to put it inside the out building where trunks were cleaned and prepared for restoration. Paula had paid extra to jump to the head of the line.

Minus unforeseen delays, turnover per trunk was two to three weeks. Jix had ample time to do a thorough job and to read Bethany's diary.

It was almost time for Earl to leave for the day but not before receiving instructions to begin on the Manikin trunk first thing the following morning. He would score and remove old canvas or paper, scrape off glue that time had hardened, and have the trunk ready for Jix to apply a cleaning solvent; a messy, time-consuming task, but one she'd done so many times she could do it blindfolded— not that she cared to.

⊶

Brrriinnnggggg! A string of shrill rings cut through the silence, jolting Abby Gayle from a state of deep slumber to sudden consciousness. She slid her sleep mask to her forehead and thrust her arm from underneath the covers to fumble for the telephone. Rising on one elbow, she held the receiver with her shoulder and managed to utter a faint hello.

"Abby Gayle, are you asleep?"

"Not anymore." She pulled the chain on the table lamp.

"Oh, I'm sorry," Jix glanced at the mantle clock. It was three quarters of an hour past midnight. "I skimmed through Bethany's diary, and I think something terrible may have happened to her."

"Why are you whispering?"

"I don't want to wake the baby or Mother. I wanted to tell you what I've discovered...actually, I didn't realize it's so late. I've lost all track of time. Sorry."

Abby Gayle swung her feet to the floor and moved across the room to her reading nook, eased onto the plump cushions of her favorite chair, and propped her bare feet on a tufted ottoman. Once she'd gotten comfortable, she rested her head against the wingback, closed her eyes, and said, "Shoot, Luke. What'd you find?"

"I didn't read it word for word; it's a five-year diary. Every page is divided into five small sections, one for each year."

"I don't understand."

"Haven't you ever seen a five-year diary?"

"No. I assume all diaries have a page for each day of a year."

"Right. Each page has five sections, one for each of five years."

"Okay. So what did she write?"

Jix glanced around the dimly lit room as if someone might be listening from the dark shadows. She whispered excitedly, "I think this Bethany person witnessed a crime or she knew something on somebody. It isn't clear from what I've read, but one thing is clear...she was terrified of someone. Here is the last entry; listen to this: *I don't know what to do. If I tell, no one will believe me. It will be my word against his. If I don't tell then he will surely kill me to keep me from talking.*"

"He who?"

11

"She doesn't say. And here's what really concerns me; before the entry I read to you, she had written she would see him at a school picnic at a lake side park, even though she didn't want to go. They were going on someone named Perry's boat, and she didn't swim. She was afraid of water. Then the rest of the pages are blank. What do you think?" Hugging the book, Jix anxiously awaited an opinion.

"I think there's nothing we can do tonight. And I think you need to get to bed. You said Paula's husband didn't go on the trip. Let's think about contacting him to see if there is a family member you might talk with for a little family history…maybe on the pretense of having something to do with decorating the inside of the trunk for the daughter. Or…here's a thought. Let sleeping dogs lie. This would have taken place decades ago. You *could* restore the trunk, collect a nice fat check, and move along to the next trunk. You could do that, you know?"

"I could," Jix thoughtfully agreed. "At least, I could try. You are probably right. It would be best to give Paula the diary and let her find out what happened to Bethany, if she even wants to know what happened to her. If anything did happen to her…."

"Go to bed. I'll talk to you tomorrow."

"Yeah. Talk to you tomorrow. Good night. Sweet dreams." Jix hung up and lingered a while before going to bed. She considered she may have overreacted. And besides, this had taken place so long ago. Taking care of her husband and her mom, helping with her granddaughter, plus running a business and a household, had her spread thin. She had no time to play detective. She should restore the trunk and get on to the next one.

Abby Gayle Kamp went to the bathroom, got a drink of water, and straightened the bed covers before she slid a sleep mask over her eyes and wiggled between the sheets.

Since she was wide-awake, she could plan what they would need to do next to determine what had happened to Bethany Perkins. She knew there not a snowball's chance in hell Jix Haynes would simply restore the trunk and let this go.

Chapter Three

On the brink of her seventy-fifth birthday, Margaret Jixson Fairmont carefully lined a Pyrex bowl with vanilla wafers, flat side down. She wanted to surprise her daughter with her favorite dessert for lunch. Margee, as she was affectionately known, cut banana slices with a paring knife at lightning-fast speed and arranged them on top of perfectly positioned wafers.

One slice of banana went to baby Dinah, happily watching her great grandmother from a wooden high chair. Her chubby little fingers let go of a sippy cup she'd been rhythmically tapping on the tray, to grasp the banana and stuff it in her mouth. Margee humored the happy little girl and put three more slices within reach, instructing her to eat one at a time.

"You are such a smart girl. You know you take after your great-grand," Margee lovingly teased. She spooned creamy, cooked vanilla custard over the bananas and wafers, added another layer of fruit, another layer of custard, and topped it all with fluffy spoonfuls of whipped meringue.

In search of her mother, Jix popped into the colorful kitchen, wallpapered in images of red and green apples spilling out of overturned baskets.

Margee cleaned Dinah's face and sticky fingers before lifting her from the high chair. Tiny, bare feet padded toward the sound of her grandmother's voice.

Jix pulled out a kitchen chair and sat down with the baby on her lap. She put the diary on the table.

"Would you mind reading this when you have time?" she asked.

Margee picked up the book. "Sure. What is it?" She thumbed through the pages.

"A diary and a photo of a young girl who owned the diary. The photo has Bethany written on the back, and the diary belonged to someone named Bethany, so I suppose the two to be one and the same. Both were in Paula Manikin's trunk, among other things. I'd like your opinion."

"About what?"

"I don't really know. Look it over, and tell me what you think. You know…overall. Watch for anything out of the ordinary. You'll have to ignore what appear to be random doodles in the margins although some are quite amusing. She has written in three colors of ink: red, green, and black. It appears to be a typical teenager's diary."

Dinah wiggled to get down and meet Willowdean, a mostly-Beagle with long, floppy ears and a nose peppered with black spots. The dog plopped down and flipped belly side up; her tail slapped the floor in three-quarter time.

"Sure, I'll be glad to read it. I'll have time this afternoon. In the meantime, set the table, and let's eat lunch. Bill will be here in about ten minutes."

"Abby Gayle is coming too. Austin is on the road. I was supposed to tell you...not that Austin is on the road, but Abby is eating with us... however, I've been busy, and it slipped my mind. Finally got the trunk cleaned; the wood is beautiful. I may not need to stain it. Sorry, I forgot about Abby Gayle coming for lunch.

"No harm done. Did Earl bring his lunch, or shall I include him?"

"I don't know. Include him, just in case."

⊶

"By Saturday, the Manikin trunk will be ready for you." Jix pumped the plunger on a bottle of lotion then rubbed her palms in a circular motion. "I dyed the straps and handles this afternoon."

Bill Haynes left a barefoot trail in the plush carpet from the bathroom to the bed. "What's to be done? And what's the hurry? Don't we have a month on this one?"

"We do."

Bill built new trays to replace missing ones and installed leather handles and straps when needed, which was almost always. Whether the situation called for replacing the floor of the trunk or broken lid hinges, Bill could handle the job. He deemed himself a trunk surgeon and the work area outside their garage as his operating room. As soon as Jix and Earl had done all they could do, Bill stepped in and added his magic touch. His day job limited his surgeon's role to nights and weekends.

17

Jix fluffed the pillow on her side of the bed before scooting under the covers and turning off the lamp. Shadowy light from a full moon dimly lit the room. She turned toward him and said to a tired, drowsy Bill, "I found a diary in the trunk."

"Good for you," he mumbled.

"Mother and I read it."

When he didn't respond, she asked, "Honey, are you listening?"

"Yes," he whispered.

"Don't you want to know who the diary belonged to and what it said?"

"It talks?"

She swatted him playfully. "Oh you! I'm serious. Mother and I both think something may have happened to a woman named Bethany. The diary belonged to her." When he didn't comment, she added, "I'm curious."

"Ask Richard."

"Who?"

"Richard Manikin. He didn't go on the trip, far as I know."

"Far as you know!" She sat upright. "Do you know these people?"

"I know Richard and his mother-in-law, Laura Riddling. We hold a mortgage in both their names."

Bill flung an arm over his eyes and pulled the sheet up under his chin when Jix jerked the chain on the bedside lamp.

"Why didn't you tell me you know the Manikins? I know you don't bring your work home, but this is ridiculous!"

Bill uncovered his eyes, squinted at his wife, and calmly said, "I didn't think it was important. Should you care to

18

launch a wild goose chase into the unknown—with what useful purpose in mind I cannot fathom in my wildest imagination—Richard's mother-in-law lives directly across the street from him. Ask her about this diary and Beverly or whatever her name is...was. But leave me out of it. Don't mention my name. You don't know me. I don't know you. We are total strangers."

"You're still mad about that one time Abby Gayle and I were arrested for trespassing, aren't you? We didn't know the antique store was closed, and we needed to verify something."

"At three-thirty in the morning?"

"That was an unfortunate incident. Anyhow, it's water under the bridge. I'm wondering about this woman. That's all. It was so long ago. I don't even know where to start."

Bill turned toward the wall and tucked the sheet under his chin. "Good night, sweetheart. Wherever your inquiring mind leads you, keep me out of it. Please call your mother if you need bail money."

Chapter Four

Richard Manikin was cordial when Jix phoned to say she wanted a graduation photo of his oldest daughter to personalize her trunk. Declaring he would leave all decorating decisions up to the ladies, he suggested she contact Paula's mother.

A call to Mrs. Riddling led to an invitation to pick up the photo. Jix would take the diary and see what, if anything, the woman knew about Bethany Perkins.

A call to Abby Gayle to see if she might want to tag along yielded an unexpected response from her friend.

"I was about to phone you. Someone has opened the box of things we took out of Paula's trunk. The tape has been cut, and the contents are scattered. I don't know when this happened."

"How did someone get in your garage?"

"I leave the door up if I go for a short walk, or I'm working in the yard, or if I go across the street to Reba Rayburn's for coffee. This is a safe neighborhood. I've never heard of a break in."

"I'm on my way over there. Do you want to go with me to talk to Paula Manikin's mother?"

"Sure. And I'll show you the box. I haven't compared the contents to my list yet. I'll be ready to go by the time you get here."

A close examination of the vandalized box raised more questions. "The shoes. Why would anyone take the high button shoes?" Jix straightened the sheet music and gathered scattered books and items.

"And the lock of hair I put in an envelope is missing." Abby Gayle circled the item on the list. "I don't think anything else was taken."

"Of all things to steal. If the thief intends to make money, he isn't thinking clearly. The things he has taken have little monetary value. The shoes are worth fifty or sixty dollars, but why take a ringlet of hair?" Jix saw tools, bicycles, and other things more likely to attract the interest of a thief. "Is anything from the garage missing?"

"No. That is the first thing I checked. This is a brand new lawn mower. If I was stealing something to sell, this would be my first choice."

The ladies discussed the situation at length. They wondered how the thief knew the trunk contents were stored in the Kamp's garage, and they concluded the intruder had only been interested in items from the trunk and nothing else. Jix remembered the black sedan she'd thought was following her. Someone could have seen them take the trunk inside. "They could have seen us bringing the box to the garage...the door was opened," Jix said.

"I suppose. It's possible they followed the trunk from Paula's to here. If so, someone is watching you and knows the trunk is now at your house."

They closed the box and taped it shut before heading to talk with Laura Riddling.

A lovely, petite lady with twinkling eyes and a friendly greeting met Jix and Abby Gayle at the door of an ordinary, yellow-brick, two-story house. There was nothing unusual about the exterior of the house located in a typical, American neighborhood in the mid-size city of Brookline.

One step onto the stone floor of Mrs. Riddling's foyer, and the girls had entered a time pocket. Dark, archaic furniture lined the plastered walls.

Mrs. Riddling escorted her guests into a small sitting room where heavy, fringed, drapes framed the windows and restricted natural light. Dark, dramatic wallpaper and old, intricately carved furniture starkly denounced current decorating trends. She gestured toward a coffee table set with a squatty teapot flanked by footed teacups.

"Shall we have tea? I'm anxious for you to try the scones. I ran across an old recipe I'd misplaced for a number of years." She sat down on an ebony settee across from the girls seated in matching his-and-hers parlor chairs.

"How nice," Jix commented, as she took a saucer cradling a cup of steaming tea. "Your home is lovely."

"Thank you, dear. I've had most of this furniture since I first married Mr. Riddling…God bless his soul."

Judging from the furnishings, one would have been justified in concluding their matrimonial union had taken place in a previous century.

Paula's mother explained she was not fond of change and had only moved to be closer to her daughter and grandchildren.

"Here is Betty Sue's graduation photo," the silver-haired lady extended a print to Jix. "I have a color photo, but I thought being as the trunk is old, this black-and-white would be more appropriate. Or would you prefer a colored one?"

"Perhaps I can take both and see which one works best."

"Good idea. You ladies enjoy a scone while I get it. Isn't Betty Sue beautiful? She favors my baby sister. Her name was Amelia; she owned the trunk for many years before leaving it to my daughter. Amelia died about three months ago."

Jix and Abby Gayle expressed their condolences; a cloud of sadness shaded her face as she turned to leave the room.

"What do you think?" Jix whispered. "Should I ask her about the diary since her sister died recently? I don't want to be insensitive."

"You know as well as I do, we're not leaving here without asking her. As to what I think about these scones–her recipe needs to be shared with the world. They are delicious." She helped herself to another.

The attractive, elderly woman presented a photo and then poured another round of tea before sitting down on the settee. Abby Gayle raved about the scones and asked if the flattered baker might share the recipe.

"It's an old family technique passed with the stipulation it remains within the family. I'm sorry, dear. I'm a bit superstitious, and I fear the worst would befall me if I broke a family tradition. We are very private people...almost to the point of secrecy," she chuckled, "but I'm glad you are enjoying them."

A matching pair of sleek, black cats, with tails like cane fishing poles stuck in a creek bank, crept in and stood aloof from the strangers. Mrs. Riddling quickly sat the remaining scones next to her and covered them with a napkin.

"They can't resist these scones. I had to close them in the bedroom upstairs when I baked, and they nearly went bonkers from the aroma." She kept a close eye on the covered scones.

Abby Gayle paused mid-chew. Only one thing came to mind that would provoke such a reaction from a cat.

Catnip.

Chapter Five

"We've taken enough of your time, Mrs. Riddling. Thank you for the tea and scones. This has been a delightful treat." Jix reached in her handbag and pulled out the diary. "Before we go…this diary was in Paula's trunk, and I am wondering if you may have known Bethany Ann Perkins." Jix opened the book and held the photo for her hostess to see.

The woman with silver hair momentarily held her breath. Her eyes no longer twinkled with merriment. Her friendly smile faded. Quickly regaining her composure, Mrs. Riddling answered, "She was my sister Amelia's friend. I didn't know her well; they were younger than my other sister and I."

"Is this Bethany Ann Perkins?" She held the photo so it could easily be seen.

Laura Riddling didn't answer.

"You said you knew her. Is this Bethany Ann Perkins?" she repeated.

"Possibly. It is an old photograph. Those old cameras didn't take very clear pictures."

"Please, Mrs. Riddling, I'd appreciate your opinion. Do you think this is Bethany Perkins?"

After a moment's hesitation, Mrs. Riddling answered, "Yes. It is Bethany Ann."

"Thank you. Do you know what happened to her? Is she still living?" Abby Gayle asked.

"No. No, I don't know. We grew up in Mississippi. After school, everyone went their separate ways. If you'll leave the diary with me, I'll give it to Paula." She moved the plate of scones from the settee to hold in her lap.

Jix slipped the photo between the pages and dropped the book in her bag. "Thank you, but I'll return it when I deliver the trunk, along with other items that now belong to Paula."

The ladies repeated their thanks for tea, excused themselves, and waved good-bye as they climbed into Jix's truck.

"What now? I think the diary is a link to something important. I'll be glad to read it to see if I can pick up on a detail you or your mother may have missed." Abby Gayle took the diary from the purse.

"Good idea. If you'll read it this afternoon, we can meet and brainstorm. Neither of us asked Mrs. Riddling which town they grew up in. We need to find out and check there for birth and death records." Jix had not a clue as to how to access such information, but she knew Bill, the mortgage guy, and he knew how to search public records.

28

They wove through light traffic, both deep in thought, until Abby Gayle's house was in sight. Jix let off the gas pedal and glanced in the rear view mirror, preparing to turn. She slid her foot from the brake to the accelerator and continued past the Kamp's driveway.

"Where are we going?" the surprised passenger asked.

"Look in your side-mirror at that black sedan behind us. I've seen it before. I think someone is following us. I strongly suspect the driver may be the same person who broke into the box."

Abby Gayle leaned to better see in the mirror. "There are lots of black cars on the road."

"Well, we're about to find out who is driving this one. Hang on!" She sped up and turned left onto a residential street. A recently repaired spare tire, loose in the truck bed, slid to the side with a bang.

The sedan also sped up.

Familiar with the streets in the neighborhood, Jix spotted a back alley and turned into the narrow, block-long, gravel trail, flanked on both sides by well-maintained back yards. The unfettered tire slid to the other side.

At the end of the alley, she slammed on the brakes, slinging the tire against the cab. Before the truck had come to a complete stop, Abby Gayle jumped out and ran behind the vehicle. A fifty-five-gallon drum used for discarded yard clippings was a challenge for a petite woman, but pushing with her hands and her knee, she toppled the metal cylinder on its side and rolled it to the middle of the road to prevent access to the street. Spinning around sharply on her heels, she dove into the seat, slammed the door, and yelled, "Go! Go! Go!"

A rush of adrenaline pulsed through Jix's veins as she stomped the accelerator. Gravel ricocheted off the overturned container.

The next block over, Jix swung into an alley running parallel to the one they'd blocked. The little truck sped to the end. Recklessly, Jix doubled back and slid to a stop. The Trunk Doctor's truck was bumper-to-bumper with an older model, black sedan.

Having left the driver's door wide open, a man wearing a baseball cap, a loose-fitting tee shirt, and jeans was rolling the barrel out of the way. The women ran around the silently, idling car to confront the surprised driver.

"Stop right there!" Jix shouted. "Why are you following me?" Before the man could answer, an accusation followed, "I know you've been tailing me. I've seen you at least three times!" Facing down the startled man, Abby Gayle stood shoulder-to-shoulder with Jix.

"Did you break into my garage? What are you after? Who are you?" Abby Gayle shouted.

Instead of answering, the tall, thin man of slight build, with dark brown eyes beneath heavy brows lunged forward. He grabbed Jix's arm and twisted it. An excruciating pain shot from her wrist to her shoulder. He spun her around, placed a hand on each shoulder, and pushed hard. Jix fell forward, knocking Abby Gayle to the ground. The man sprinted to his car, jumped in, and slammed the door.

"He's going to run over us. Hurry, Abby! Hurry!" Trying to gain traction, Jix scrambled, getting her bearings.

She jumped to her feet and clung to her friend as they struggled to stand. The two dove to safety in the nick of time but not before the front fender grazed Abby Gayle, forcefully thrusting her against a picket fence. She collapsed and slid to the ground.

Screeching tires howled as rubber gripped asphalt. Within seconds, the car was out of sight.

"Are you all right?" Jix swallowed a broken sob. She crawled on her hands and knees to Abby Gayle. Brushing her friend's hair to expose a knot swelling to the size of a golf ball, she helped her to a sitting position.

Abby Gayle leaned back against the fence and blinked, in an effort to stave off unconsciousness. A trail of blood trickled from a cut above her eye. Her knees were skinned and bleeding.

"I think so." Abby Gayle reached in her pocket for a tissue to blot the bleeding cut. A quick check acknowledged Jix's scraped elbows and bruised knees as the sum-total of her injuries.

"Can you stand up? See if you can move. I think we should go to the emergency room and let them check you over…be sure nothing is broken or out of place."

Already feeling the ache of her injuries, the wounded woman flexed her arms and legs. "I'm fine, a bit banged up. Nothing's broken. No doubt I'll be sore from head to toe. And I need to get ice on this hatching goose egg." She gently touched the rising bump on her forehead with her fingertips.

With the aid of the wooden fence, she pulled herself to her feet. Each steadying the other, they hobbled to the truck.

"We have to find out who he is and what he wants. This has something to do with the trunk and the diary. I think I'll read the diary again and see if I can find a clue." After helping her friend into the truck, Jix went around

31

and slid in the driver's seat, wincing when she bent her skinned elbows.

"I can read it tonight since I'll have to cancel my plans to run in the marathon," Abby Gayle sarcastically commented. "I also will need to think of an explanation for Austin when he gets home tomorrow night as to why I appear to have taken part in a gang fight."

"We need to report this to the police. The man assaulted us then attempted to run over us! You've had a break-in and a robbery! Let's get you home and cleaned up; then I'll call the police." She sighed before adding, "Bill isn't going to be happy...not even a little bit."

"Ask for the woman cop who interviewed us when we had that little mishap at the antique store." Abby Gayle's skinned knees were burning as if they were on fire. She was anxious to clean the wounds and apply a soothing ointment.

"What was her name?"

Holding her hand to her forehead, Abby Gayle found it difficult to think. "The only reason I remember is it's an unusual name. Bird. Her name is Something Bird."

"Only person I ever knew named Bird is a Civil War officer. Colonel Thompson Bird Lamar. I didn't know him personally; I read about him. Not that it has anything to do with anything," Jix digressed. Her mind was wandering, and her temples were pounding.

Both women recalled the time they'd met a policewoman in her early forties with coal black eyes, short, black hair, and beautiful, flawless skin the color of latte.

"It doesn't matter about her first name. I'll ask for Officer Bird. I'll bet there's only one."

32

Chapter Six

As luck would have it, Officer Bird was on duty when Jix phoned. Officer Avonelle Stelana Bird, that is.

The women had met under tense circumstances when a tripped alarm at the Sixth Avenue Antique Store summoned the police. A misunderstanding had been unraveled and inadvertently triggered what would eventually become, both personally and professionally, firm friendships rooted in trust and admiration.

Officer Bird suppressed a chuckle as the incident came to mind. She advised they err on the side of caution and talked both women into going to the emergency room for a proper examination, promising to meet them there.

Abby Gayle fussed but followed Jix. Citing that Jix's truck had not been designed with comfort in mind, she insisted they take her car as soreness set in. Her aching body demanded decent shock absorbers for a smoother ride, as well as upholstered seats to help cushion her pain.

X-rays and a thorough examination disclosed zero life-threatening issues and gave Abby Gayle an I-told-you-so moment. Officer Bird and the ladies retreated to a room the hospital had designated as a chapel or prayer room.

Abby Gayle settled back on a sofa in the sparsely furnished room and purposed to ignore the steady drumming sensation in her head until the medication she'd been given could bring relief. Jix, her elbows swabbed and bandaged, had gotten three sodas from a vending machine.

Officer Bird's gentle but no-nonsense manner put the ladies at ease. They rehashed their first meeting, laughing about the awkward situation six months earlier. Miscommunication between the girls and an antique storeowner had them thinking they had permission to go inside the store when they didn't. Jix reminded them, "That's water under the bridge."

With pen poised over a pocket-sized notebook, Avonelle S. Bird crossed her trouser-clad legs and proceeded with the interview. Beginning from when Ernest unlocked Paula's trunk, Jix and Abby recounted the events concerning the trunk and the diary up to the time of their near demise. They described the man and his car.

"Would you recognize this man if you saw him again?"

Jix nodded her head. "I know I would."

"Me too," Abby Gayle answered, deliberately avoiding nodding her head.

"Did he have any distinguishing features…a scar, a tattoo, a beard, or mustache? Anything unusual?"

Both women answered no. Then Jix added, "Would heavy eyebrows count? He has dark brown eyes. Dark hair. Everything happened so fast, but I would recognize him."

Bird jotted down the observation before adding, "Sleep on it. You never know; something else may come to mind. Come to the station in the morning, and we'll have a composite sketch artist do a drawing while the man's face is fresh in your mind. Say...eight o'clock? Is that too early?"

"Works for me," Abby Gayle said. "I have a lot to do tomorrow; if I'm able to get out of bed." She managed a chuckle although a painful one.

"I'll come and get you," Jix spoke to Abby Gayle.

"In the meantime, I'll check on a few things and get back to you ladies." Officer Bird clicked her pen and stuck it in her shirt pocket. She then leaned forward and said, "Off the record and jus' among the three of us, I don't take to nobody runnin' over women in any form or fashion. We gonna look under every rock till we find this lowlife."

Straightening up and switching on her professional tone of voice, the policewoman tipped her cap and said, "Nice to see you girls again. Go home, and get some rest now. See you in the morning."

⚷

"Come join us, Carol."

Jix made drinks and opened a new package of chocolate chip cookies she'd put on the kitchen table beside a big bowl of buttered popcorn. Carol appeared, pulled out a chair, said, "Catch me up," and plopped down.

While they'd waited for her to put Dinah to bed, Abby Gayle had shared with Jix and Margee details of the anniversary dinner she and Austin had enjoyed at a five star restaurant, even the part about how determined she'd been not to allow her aching body to spoil their special day. The celebratory occasion had helped soften her husband's shock and anger of returning home to find his wife battered and bruised.

Bill and Austin retired to the den with popcorn and drinks to watch an Atlanta/Houston game. The women were anxious to discuss Bethany's journal.

Folding back the cover on a notebook, Abby Gayle jotted down the date on the top line. Ready to take notes, she opened the discussion with a query aimed at no one in particular. "Did anything in particular grab your attention as you read the diary?"

"Well, I wondered about the nightmares," Margee popped a kernel of popped corn in her mouth. "Was she writing about a dream or something she had witnessed?"

Abby Gayle noted Margee's question.

Carol put two cookies on a napkin. She scooted her chair back and went to get a jar of peanut butter out of the cabinet and a knife from the drawer.

As she unscrewed the top to the jar, she said, "It's a five-year diary although she didn't complete five years. The nightmares were near the end. If she'd written about them in the beginning, when she was younger, I might think of them as being bad dreams. But because she was older...and it is plain to see maturity in her writing as the years went by...I'm inclined to think she is talking about something she actually experienced rather than dreamed."

Jix picked up the diary and fanned the pages, "Even her handwriting matured over the years. This is eerie. We don't know this person, yet we've seen her grow. To answer your question, Abby, there are several things I can't get past. I've gone over and over them. There is the entry I read to you. She indicated she was afraid of someone.

36

Something about her word against his, and she was concerned if he knew she knew whatever was dangerous to know, this person might do her bodily harm."

Abby Gayle wrote as Jix spoke.

"That is thought provoking," Carol commented, "but nothing I read stated unequivocally anything harmful happened to Bethany or there was ever a crime."

Margee agreed, "I didn't read anything that made me think a crime had actually been committed. She was a young girl overreacting as young girls are prone to do." She glanced at Carol before adding, "Not all young girls, of course."

Carol pointed with the blade of the butter knife, "Who is R.V.Q.?" She spread peanut butter on the cookies. "Anybody want milk?" she asked on her way to the refrigerator.

"Make that beer." Austin, followed by Bill, came into the kitchen. Carol sat the milk on the counter and handed two bottles of beer to sandy-haired, six-foot-five, Austin. He flashed a handsome, boyish grin and passed Bill a bottle. Standing behind his wife who was seated at the table, he put his hands on Abby Gayle's shoulders. While gently massaging her sore muscles, he spotted the diary.

"My sister Pam had a diary very similar to this one. I got the whuppin' of a lifetime when I read it and told anybody who would listen what she'd written." He chuckled as he reached over his wife and picked up the book.

"Yep. Hers was like this. You do know it has a secret pocket, don't you?"

Collectively a cry of "secret pocket" rose.

"Shhhh! Don't wake the baby," Carol cocked one ear toward the nursery to listen for Dinah's cry.

37

Bill stepped up. "For Pete's sake, don't encourage them, Austin. It's time for the game to start; we'd better get back in there."

"Believe me, the last thing I want to do is encourage them. My better half has promised to not take any more chances. No two ways about it, y'all need to mind your own business." He swept his eyes around the circle of women indicating his advice applied to each of them. "I'm just saying, if this diary is the same as Pam's, it has a secret compartment. Where's the key?"

"It's open," Jix pointed out the obvious.

"The secret pocket isn't. Do you have a key?"

Margee moved the peanut butter jar and picked up the key, dangling from a narrow, pink ribbon.

Austin inserted it in the lock. "You turn it counter-clockwise twice, if I remember how hers worked."

Click. Click.

The back cover popped open exposing four, thin, cleverly concealed blank pages. An envelope, tucked between the pages, dislodged and fell to the floor.

Chapter Seven

Austin stooped to retrieve the envelope as the ladies observed in disbelief. Bill went to the den to watch the ball game.

"Oh my goodness; of all things!" Jix exclaimed. Austin handed her the envelope.

"Exactly like Pam's. When we were kids, it took me a while to discover if there were secret compartments, but I lucked out. My buddy Jimmy had figured out how to unlock his sister's diary." He shook with laughter, remembering how wickedly amusing it had been to expose his sister's secrets, making it worth the price he'd paid when his Mother discovered what he'd done.

"Oh, my," Margee exclaimed, glad she'd raised two girls who got along...most of the time. "Did she ever forgive you for invading her privacy?"

"I doubt it. She still brings it up occasionally, jokingly now, not so back then, when she was fit to be tied. The more she cried, the madder Momma got. I think Daddy was on my side, but he couldn't say so. To get even, Miss Goody Two Shoes started a rumor about me I don't care to think about, much less discuss." He patted Abby Gayle's shoulder. "I'd better get back to the ball game. I'll check later to see what's in the envelope."

Jix turned the letter-size, sealed envelope over; a decoratively designed monogram was stamped on the flap. Carol jumped to her feet and hurried to the den, her words trailing over her shoulder, "I'll get a letter opener, Mom."

All eyes were fixed on Jix as she slid the blade under the flap. Carefully slicing the old paper, she extracted a single sheet of stationery monogrammed with a decorative B.

Abby Gayle leaned near to get a better view. Margee and Carol peered over Jix's shoulder.

"It's a bunch of numbers. This makes no sense," Carol said, as they hovered close to inspect five, neatly printed rows of numbers.

"A code," Abby Gayle surmised.

"No doubt," Margee concurred.

Abby Gayle grabbed her notebook and pen. "I can give us each a copy to study." Always the organizer, she presented a sensible plan.

Jix called each number line-by-line as Abby Gayle wrote them down.

A. 53122
B. 61853
C. 57214
D. 92955
E. 5762

"Could be anything," Margee said. "She was a teenager when she wrote this. Maybe it was a secret code she shared with a friend or something. We don't need to rack our brains trying to figure this out; it is most likely nothing. Kid's play."

"Mother's right," Jix said. "This is probably some silly thing she did to have something hidden. She had a big secret; only it wasn't about anything that mattered. We all know how kids pretend."

Carol sat down and buttered another cookie with peanut butter. "Are we forgetting she wasn't a child? She was what...seventeen or eighteen when the last entry was written? That's a little old to be playing Nancy Drew games."

Jix muttered more to herself than to the others, "And we have to consider the things she wrote about seeing something or being afraid of someone."

Abby Gayle had written the code five times. "Where are the scissors?" she asked. Carol took shears from the knife block and handed them to her.

She gave each person a list of the numbers. Silence settled over the group as each pondered what the list represented, if anything.

A rafter-rattling shout came from the den.

"Atlanta won," Abby Gayle said. "Good, the game's over. We need to get home; it's getting late."

Two happy Braves' fans breezed into the kitchen. Bill lifted the lid on the recycle bin and deposited the empty glass bottles.

Austin, riding a winner's high, turned to the ladies and gleefully asked, "What is in the envelope?"

41

Abby Gayle held up her noted numbers.

"Numbers. Could be a code or something. Or could be nothing at all."

He examined the paper before handing it to Bill, who'd pulled up a backless stool and parked his backside on it.

"Get the other stool," Bill said to Austin.

"We need to go." Abby Gayle began to clean up stray popcorn from her placemat. Austin reached over and dipped his hand into the popcorn bowl adding more strays to be captured. He lifted a stepstool tucked in the corner, careful to not awaken Willowdean from a doggie snooze, and sat down.

Margee asked, "What do you think? Did you learn to break codes when you were a boy?"

Austin chuckled. "Not really. I ordered a secret decoder one time off a cereal box."

"How long are you home?" Carol stifled a yawn. She glanced at the apple-shaped clock with seeds for numerals. It was past her bedtime, and as reliable as the clock on the wall, Dinah woke at five each morning ready for breakfast and a dry diaper. As Carol listened to Austin's answer, she put the cookies away and loaded the glasses and cups in the dishwasher.

"A few more days. I have a big load to take to California with several stops along the way. I'll be gone ten days if everything goes according to plans."

"I don't know how you two manage being apart so much, but you seem to have mastered it," Jix said.

"Driving eighteen-wheelers is what I do. We make it work for us." Austin credited his partner who orchestrated their lives to harmonize with his job.

With the table cleared, Abby Gayle gathered her things to leave. Everyone was standing except Bill. He sat on the stool studying the scrap of paper he held.

"What years are the diary?" he addressed his question to Jix.

"Fifty-two through fifty-seven. June of fifty-seven."

"Every line has a fifty number in it. Fifty-three, fifty-seven, fifty-five. That's the key to the code."

The women found their scraps of paper and thought-out the numbers.

"So, what, Daddy?" Carol asked.

"So it could be the year. And the other numbers could be the month and day. A on the list could be January 22, 1953. B could be June 18, 1953, and so on."

"Even so, what does it mean?" Margee wondered.

"Give me the diary, honey." Jix handed him the book.

Bill scrolled through mental algorithms before he turned to entries made on January 22nd. "Somebody write this down."

Abby Gayle set her pocketbook on the table and opened her notebook, prepared to write.

"On January 22nd all words are written in black ink, with the exception of one. The word *I* is written in green ink. Actually, it is traced over with green ink; it was originally written in black ink. Write down I," he said to Abby Gayle.

Jix said, "She did this throughout the book. Some words she wrote in red ink, some green; most are black. I assumed she had colored ink and an artistic flair."

Deep in thought, he thumbed to B on the list. "On June 18, 1953, the green word is *saw*." She jotted the word down.

Everyone gathered close as Bill found entry C. "*Bobby* is the next word."

"Fourth word is *drown*." There were startled gasps and expressions of alarm. Jix grabbed her mother's hand and held it tight.

He searched for the last word. "And the final word is *Roselyn*."

Although there was no need to repeat the sentence, Abby Gayle read it, "I saw Bobby drown Roselyn."

Bill closed the diary and handed it to his wife. An ear-to-ear smile flashed across his face. He rose from the stool, pounded his good buddy Austin on the back, shook hands, and wished him a safe trip.

"That was some game, wasn't it!" he exclaimed. "Please excuse me folks. I hate to decipher and run, but I'm going to bed. Good-night all." He gave Jix a quick kiss on the cheek, immediately followed by the sound of the bedroom door closing.

Chapter Eight

The next day, Jix contacted Officer Bird with the new information.

Told they would need to examine the diary, Jix, not being the owner of the book, felt she should contact Paula or her husband to let them know what had transpired, and to get permission to relinquish the diary. Richard Manikin had returned her call to say he had an hour to spare if she could come to his office at ten.

After a twenty-minute wait, he emerged to greet his guest. Richard, a tall man with an athletic build, was dressed in gray slacks and a short-sleeved dress shirt and tie. Jix was surprised. She had expected someone closer to Paula's age. Jolly as a Christmas elf, he extended his hand, "Mrs. Haynes, how nice to meet you."

She shook hands and replied, "Please call me Jix. Thank you for your time; I know you're busy."

He motioned toward a chair facing his desk and went around to his cushioned swivel chair. Scattered across the top of the bookcases behind him, pretty Paula and all five Manikin daughters beamed a happy family image from a montage of photographs.

"How's Betty Sue's trunk coming along? I hope you've not come for advice. I know nothing about what she and her mother have in mind. I just write the checks," he quipped.

Jix was amused. Paula had already paid for the trunk restoration with a check she'd written. "No, I've not come about trunk restoration. We've cleaned and prepared the trunk for Bill. He does all the repairs. He'll start on it soon."

"I've heard he's quite handy with tools."

The owner of a well-established car dealership spread over an acre glanced at his watch, prompting his visitor to get to the point, albeit she'd waited on him.

"I've come about an item found in the trunk."

"Oh? How so?"

"There were many things inside. As you may know, the trunk was locked, and it is my understanding it had been locked for a number of years. Paula said she inherited it from her aunt."

"She did; her mother's youngest sister. Aunt Amelia died tragically a few months ago. I can't say why Paula was the recipient of the trunk, but nevertheless, a trucking company delivered it to us. It arrived on the heels of Betty Sue's graduation. Paula wanted to keep the trunk in the family and thought it would be a gift our daughter would appreciate and cherish."

46

"May I ask where Aunt Amelia lived?"

"Jackson, Mississippi. Paula's family is from there…or that area."

"What was Aunt Amelia's last name…if you don't mind me asking?"

"Not at all. Adams. Amelia Adams. Why the questions?"

Jix pulled the diary from her purse and passed it across the desk to Richard Manikin. She explained how her initial concern had culminated into the coded note hidden in a secret compartment. She left out the part about how Bill had deciphered the note, as well as the part about a close call with a man who'd broken into and stolen trunk items. She told him she'd talked with someone at the police department, and they'd asked to examine the diary.

Richard expressed a willingness to cooperate in any way. Jix sought to read his response, thus concluding the man appeared to be intrigued.

"Have you ever heard of Bethany Ann Perkins?"

"Not that I recall. I wonder if she is a family member, perhaps a cousin. Paula's family is not close. As a matter of fact, Paula hadn't seen this aunt for many years. She visited her a few times in the summer when she was a child. She told me this when the trunk first arrived. My dear wife was puzzled as to why she inherited the trunk. She hardly remembered the woman." He looked at the photo and then handed it and the diary back. "If anyone should have inherited it, the person most likely would be Paula's mother. As I've said, she was Amelia's sister. You should ask her."

"I did."

Richard's eyebrows rose to his hairline. "What did she say?"

"Not much. She did appear to be a little shaken when I showed her the diary. Mrs. Riddling offered to give it to Paula if I'd leave it with her. And she identified the girl in the photo as Bethany, so she knew her personally."

"Is this Bethany alive today?" He did a quick mental tally. "She could be. If this took place thirty years ago, and she looks to be...say...twenty, then today, she would be in her fifties, or there about."

"The police will surely check birth and death records," Jix said.

"You'd think, however, considerable time has passed. The police have more pressing cases, and this may be put on hold. I'll talk to Paula sometime today, taking into consideration the time difference. I don't want to upset her; they are having a pleasant trip, so I'll tell her we talked, and you've unlocked the trunk."

"She may ask what was inside, and then you can tell her about the diary. Ask if she knows of Bethany Ann Perkins."

Jix genuinely liked Richard Manikin. He was charismatically typical of sales people at a high-end dealership. She guessed him to be in his late fifties, better than average looking, with smiling brown eyes. Photos atop the bookcase revealed he was a man who lived in a house with six women.

"I'll call you if my wife knows anything about the diary or its owner. After I talk to Paula, you know there's a big time difference to take into account," he repeated, as if to remind himself, "and see what information she contributes. I'll have our girl who processes legal contracts find out if this Bethany is dead or alive—she can search records in Jackson."

"Thank you so much. With your permission, I'm on my way to give the diary to Officer Bird."

"Avonelle Bird?" he asked.

"One and the same," Jix smiled. "We've met on more than one occasion. She's sharp as a tack and very likable."

With a reminiscent gleam in his eye, he said, "Avonelle and I go back a long way. She is indeed very likeable, and although she's both capable and professional, she is open to suggestions. I'll talk with our lady cop tomorrow and let you know if I find out anything new. In the meantime, why don't you call again on my mother-in-law? She's been down in the dumps the last few days. She may be missing Paula and the girls. Your visit is certain to cheer her."

I'm not so certain, thought Jix. *My recent visit may well be the reason she's down in the dumps.*

Chapter Nine

A few days passed and not a word from Richard. It had occurred to Jix, perhaps, he had been *too* anxious to help. The longer she waited, the more she doubted his sincerity. Maybe he knew more than he'd told. Aware she was prone to second-guess first impressions, she filed doubts away and purposed to remain positive. He was a good-natured man. She told herself Richard Manikin was genuinely interested in finding out what had become of Bethany Ann.

Austin was back on the road, and Abby Gayle had an antiquing trip on her mind. Jix wondered if her friend was aware that each time her husband left, she launched an antique buying venture, which had at times spanned several states. The woman found bargains worth driving to the ends of the earth to claim. She was a wheeler-dealer, a sharp buyer, and knowledgeable when it came to antiques.

51

"I can't get away," Jix peeped out the window at a wall of trunks waiting for a second chance. She told Abby Gayle over the phone, "Mother's birthday is coming up, and I have to make plans for a get-together. Earl hasn't felt well. He left early yesterday, and Bill and I had to take up the slack; we worked till midnight. I wallpapered a small camelback while Bill polished metal on Paula's trunk."

"Well, let's do a day trip. Let's get an early start and go to a little town just over the state line. I've been meaning to ride over there and look around a bit. We can hit the antique stores, eat lunch…there's a tearoom that comes highly recommended…and be back by late afternoon. Isn't Carol off work tomorrow?"

"Yes, she is." Jix hesitated.

She needed to take a day off about as much as she needed a hole in the roof, but a day spent junking around was tempting. The thrill of a hunt beckoned, even though neither woman needed another stick of furniture or another do-dad to gather dust.

Abby Gayle bought for herself, but Jix bought fixer-upper furniture and resold it in a rented stall at an antique mall where legions of dealers and multifarious old things stirred sentimental longings or wistful affections for the past. The antique mall was usually crowded, especially on weekends, but most shoppers were strolling down memory lane, not buying.

This venture had yet to turn a profit. Every now and then, Jix sold enough to cover her rent, but for the most part, selling in an antique mall had not proven to be a lucrative endeavor. Still, she bought and hoped to sell, as if she didn't have enough to do.

"Okay," she relented. "What time should I be ready?"

"Seven too early?"

"No. Let's stop at Hardee's for a steak and biscuit."

"Sounds good. See you in the morning."

Jix was ready when a little trailer tagging behind a white Suburban rolled to a stop at the end of her driveway. The vehicle was an older model, but in good running condition; perfect for pulling a trailer and transporting everything from chairs to glass chandeliers. The trailer hitched to her SUV came in handy when she found a bargain too large to fit inside the vehicle.

Dressed in jeans and layered shirts in anticipation of rising temperatures, the two wound their way along a two-lane highway, merrily munching biscuits and sipping coffee.

"Richard Manikin called last night." Jix wadded the biscuit wrapper and stuck it in the sack it had come in. "I didn't call you because it was late, and I knew I'd see you this morning."

Handing over her wrapper to be discarded, the driver asked, "What'd he have to say?"

"He's talked to Paula several times since the day I met with him. He didn't want to upset her and put a damper on her trip, so he gathered little bits of information on each phone call."

Jix drank the last of her coffee and put the Styrofoam cup in the sack, rolled the top of the paper bag down, and brushed crumbs from her lap.

"Does she know Bethany?" A flip of the visor deflected the morning sun.

"She has seen photos of Amelia and Bethany in an album."

"Does she know where this album is now?"

"I'm not sure. This is second-hand information. But Richard did say his Girl Friday checked records in Jackson and found a birth certificate for Bethany but no record of her death. I'll bet she's still alive. Wish I knew how to find her."

"Did you give the diary to Officer Bird?"

"Yes, I did. She said they would investigate. We'll see. They haven't been able to find the black sedan or a man fitting our description of the driver. I think we need to visit Laura Riddling again. She knows what we need to know. We have to figure out how to get it out of her."

"If I go with you, I'm not eating anything."

Jix laughed. "We mustn't be impolite."

Upon reaching Springhill, a two-century-old town with a population of less than nine hundred, the girls rode down tree-lined Main Street where flower baskets overflowing with blooming annuals waved a welcome from vintage light posts.

They crept at a snail's pace past a fifties ice cream shop, a florist, an awning-shaded bookstore, four or five antique stores, and Burwell's Hardware, where a poker-faced, six-foot tall, wooden Indian guarded the entrance. The narrow street with parallel parking looped back at a roundabout in front of an ancient train depot turned tearoom. A sign hung near the entrance that read *All Aboard, It's Tea Time.*

Abby Gayle parked the trailer near the depot in a vacant lot. They walked back, stopping at the first antique store. Nothing screamed out "take me with you," so they went on to the hardware store, marveling at items their grandmothers had used—tin biscuit cutters and washboards and kerosene lamps.

Jix bought a galvanized tin washboard to hang in her kitchen with plans to use magnets to hold notes. She'd said to Abby Gayle, "who in the world buys this junk?" when the idea hit her.

After a browse through the bookstore and a look through a second-hand furniture store, the women lucked up on a Murphy bed Abby Gayle set her sights on. The antique dealer sensed she had a serious buyer and negotiations began.

The dealer, a thin woman with stringy hair twisted and pinned in the back, peered at the shoppers through large, round, horn-rimmed specs that made her look like a frightened owl.

"You know how this all began?" she chuckled, and then answered her own question. "Probably not. The story goes, Old William Murphy had an opera singer for a lady friend, and he lived in a one-room apartment. I think this was in San Francisco or somewhere likewise." She paused trying to remember where Mr. Murphy had resided although it didn't matter in the least.

"The moral code of the time frowned upon a lady being in a man's bedroom." She paused to catch her breath, "So he converted the room into a parlor. Only thing was, he needed a place to sleep. He invented a bed that would fold up and stand against the wall. Designed it to look like a piece of parlor furniture." She laughed. "It's just like a man to find a way to pursue his interest, if you catch my drift."

The ladies politely smiled.

Jix wandered over to a display case to give Abby Gayle room to close the deal. She admired a collection of fountain ink pens on display, wondering if any were like the ink pen Bethany had used to write in her diary.

Abby Gayle unfolded the bed and commented she would need to have a new mattress custom-made. The dealer suggested a mattress cover, a sheet, and let it go…the bed was so uncomfortable no human being could sleep on it, she implied. Even so, the seller cut the price a hundred dollars. The buyer pulled out three crisp bills and fanned them. She laid the money on the bed—a hundred dollars less than the hundred-dollar discount—and gave the owl-eyed woman a take-it-or-leave-it nod.

The dealer took it. Abby Gayle paid and made arrangements to get the bed on her way out of town. The elated owner of a bed she would have to find room for, she offered to buy lunch, and off the two headed for the train station tearoom.

Chapter Ten

One of the two original waiting rooms inside the brick building, parallel to a section of iron rails leading nowhere, now served as a gift shop, the other as a dining room. Baggage claim and the ticket office had become dining areas decorated with vintage semaphores. Railroad photographs and artifacts depicting railroad history were displayed on every wall.

The luggage room housed a museum showcasing the town's founding and growth history, as well as the contribution of the railroad to the town. Owners of the tearoom resided in the stationmaster's old living quarters.

Specials for the day were listed on a blackboard where once train schedules had been penned in chalk and updated with the swipe of an eraser.

And best of all, an audio system played background noises of day-to-day activities in train depots of the past. The arrival and boarding of trains was announced over the sound of rhythmic clicks made by a telegrapher tapping out telegram messages in Morse code.

"This is amazing!"

Jix and Abby Gayle reveled in the ambience of a faded, golden age. Steamboats and river traffic had lost out to the rise of superior, faster, more reliable trains. Ironically, in due time, airlines and interstates had replaced rail traffic.

Nancy—according to her nametag—seated the ladies at a round table-for-two draped in a white, linen table skirt.

"This is exciting! I can imagine we're traveling by train. We have our tickets, we've checked our luggage, and we're waiting," Jix said, as an approaching train was broadcast over the audio system. "Nope, not our train. Listen for the next one," she pretended.

"This is such fun! Why haven't we heard of this place before now?" Abby Gayle unfolded a cloth napkin and spread it in her lap.

Jix read the menu on the blackboard. "I think I have heard of it; I didn't realize what we were missing. Look at the menu." Resigned to a choice of quiche or salad, Jix was surprised to find in addition to typical tearoom fare, hot lunches were served.

"It has been ages since I've eaten a hot roast beef sandwich. I think I'll order one." As an afterthought, she added, "I hope the mashed potatoes are made with real potatoes, not instant."

"Make it two," Abby Gayle said to Nancy, who had arrived with two glasses of water.

"The potatoes are real. Cole slaw?"

"Sure, why not?" Jix answered.

"Gravy on the mashed potatoes?" The young waitress with delightful dimples scribbled on a green pad.

"Extra gravy for me," Jix said. "And bring a bottle of ketchup, please."

"Same here, although I won't need ketchup." As one is prone to do, Abby Gayle preferred her gravy without ketchup.

Although both were left with little room for dessert, they ordered a Train Yard Trifle—layers upon layers of fruit, custard, and crumbled almond cookies, crowned with fluffy whipped cream, and drizzled with caramel and toasted almonds. It was too tempting to resist.

Full, satisfied, and content, the friends left the tearoom and leisurely strolled toward the SUV. The temperature had risen to a pleasant seventy-seven. It was early summer in the mountains; that perfect, but all too brief, period of time right before winter's bitter cold is rivaled by summer's sweltering heat.

Suddenly taken by surprise, Jix gasped, grabbed her companion's arm, and ducked for cover behind the nearest tree. Before a startled Abby Gayle could speak, Jix crouched and scurried toward a van parked near the depot, towing her clueless counterpart by the arm.

"What? What are you doing?"

"Don't look! No, do look...don't let them see you."

"Who? Where?" Abby Gayle pried Jix's hand off her arm. "If you don't mind!" She brushed her sleeve.

Peeping around the vehicle, Jix pointed down Main Street. Abby Gayle followed suit, using the van for cover.

"There," she pointed with her index finger. "Those two men in front of the hardware store. Beside the wooden Indian...do you see them?"

"Yeah. So?"

"It's the guy who tried to run over us!" Jix whispered as loud as a whisper can be before it is no longer a whisper.

Chapter Eleven

Abby Gayle craned her neck to get a better view of the
two men engaged in conversation. "I suppose it could be.
Looks like the same ball cap or one like it. Hard to tell."

"There's a black car parked across the street from the
hardware store. Could be the one the police are looking
for. We have to get a closer look." Jix once again grabbed
Abby Gayle's arm. She shook loose.

"Are you crazy? And do what? We should go back in
the tearoom and call the police."

"He could be gone by then...if it is the same man.
Follow me. Stay low, and let's go around this way and get
under the bookstore awning. The door is recessed; we can
hide in the alcove."

"No. They'll see us, and if it is the same man, he'll run
just as he did before."

"They aren't going to see us. Act casual. Come on,
follow me, and keep your head down."

Abby Gayle jerked Jix's shirttail as she started toward the bookstore. "Wait! Wait! Let's get to the Suburban, and then we'll drive past the hardware store. They're talking; they won't pay any attention to us. You get a good look as we go by, and be certain it is the same fellow."

Jix considered the suggestion of a safer option.

"Okay. Let's go." She clutched a bag holding a toddler-sized tee shirt she'd bought for Dinah in the tearoom gift shop.

They walked casually toward Abby Gayle's vehicle. Once inside, Jix relaxed a bit, feeling more in control of the situation. At least this time they were in a better position to do the *running over*, should the occasion call for such action, which she sincerely hoped it would not.

Abby Gayle had parked so there was no need to back the trailer. She pulled forward and cautiously wove her way into the roundabout traffic. Once through the circular drive, she followed close behind a car inching down the main thoroughfare.

As they approached the hardware store, Jix shielded her face with her arm propped in the window. The men were laughing and talking, neither noticing the traffic.

"It's him. I'd swear to it in court." She looked away.

As the Suburban neared the antique store, Abby Gayle slowed to a stop. She waved her hand out the window in a circular motion for a car behind to come around.

"The dealer said to load from an alley in back of the store." She continued to signal for cars to pull around.

"You go on. I'll keep an eye on these two." And before Abby Gayle could object, Jix hopped out and slammed the door.

Once Abby Gayle had located the alley and parked near the store's loading ramp, she saw the Murphy bed outside waiting to be claimed. Leaving her vehicle and trailer parked so they didn't block the narrow, gravel back road, she went inside the store.

It took a few minutes to locate the woman with round spectacles. When she came from a back room munching a donut, Abby Gayle promised to return shortly and then hurried out the front door.

Two doors down from Burwell's Hardware she spotted Jix. Rushing to her side, Abby Gayle whispered, "Are they still there?"

"They're across the street." She motioned toward the man they'd recognized. "Over there." He sat behind the steering wheel of a familiar black sedan. His companion leaned near, conversing through the open window.

"What's the plan? Please tell me we have one," Abby Gayle asked.

"Looks like his friend is staying behind. Let's follow him. With any luck, we can strike up a conversation and find out who he is."

"Why not? And maybe Miss Owl Lady will load the bed onto my trailer while we're exercising our social skills," she sarcastically commented.

The sedan pulled out, blended into traffic, and was soon a dot in the distance. The man left behind crossed the street and walked briskly in their direction, sidestepping shoppers as he made his way along the busy sidewalk.

The girls high-tailed it to the antique store and waited near the door for the well-built—otherwise nondescript—fellow dressed in Western wear. Abby Gayle hailed him as he neared.

"Excuse me, Sir," she said. "I'm from out of town, and I've purchased a Murphy bed from this antique store," she tossed her head toward her shoulder. "It's too heavy for us to load on a trailer. Would you be interested in making a few bucks? We need someone to help."

Jix added, "If not, we understand. We don't know anyone in town. We're hoping to find someone who can help us."

The man had a kind face and a pleasant demeanor. "Don't they have someone who loads and delivers? Most furniture and antique stores do."

"I think so. While we ate lunch, someone moved it to the loading ramp, but when we came back, I only saw the owner. She's a tiny woman. Doesn't look strong at all. We need to get on the road to get home before dark." Abby Gayle strove to sound needy. She looked to Jix for support.

"We're on a tight schedule," Jix quickly took up the cause. "We can't wait for her helper to return."

"Sure, I'll be glad to do what I can. Where is it?"

Abby Gayle led the way straight through the store to the alley. Jix lagged behind to tell the dealer they didn't need anyone to help with the bed, in case her employee was there.

The man suggested Abby Gayle pull the trailer closer to the ramp. While they waited, Jix asked, "Do you live here?"

"In the area."

He wasn't as talkative as Jix would have liked. She gabbed about how surprised they'd been to discover such a lovely little town and especially the transformed train depot.

"Do you eat there often? If so, I highly recommend the hot roast beef sandwich."

Abby Gayle parked the trailer even with the ramp and joined the others before the man could answer. Jix said to her friend, "This nice man lives in the area."

Ignoring them both, the polite but indifferent recruit said, "If you two will grab hold of one side, I can get the other. We need to keep it from tipping over. Looks like the rollers are useless. One is broken."

The women did as instructed. The bed, the size of a doublewide refrigerator, weighed a ton.

All were aware they were handling an antique and considered the possibility the hinges had weakened. If so, it could flop open. Placing the heavy load on the trailer turned out to be the easier part of the task. Tilting it backwards and lowering it to lie flat was a feat requiring both strength and balance. Once the deed was done, the women and the volunteer, who'd had no idea what he was getting into or he would have declined, sat down on the trailer. The man pulled a red bandana from his back pocket and mopped his face.

"We couldn't have managed without you." Abby Gayle took a ten-dollar bill from her wallet and handed it to him. "Thanks a million," she said.

Nodding appreciatively, he took it. "Glad to help. I should apply here if they need a helper."

"Are you working now?" Jix jumped on an opportunity to pry.

"I'm between jobs. We just moved here."

"We? Are you married?" Abby Gayle retrieved a wad of bungee cords from inside the SUV.

"No. I live with a friend. We recently moved here," he repeated, as he slid off the trailer and stood to leave.

"We don't even know your name." Jix took one end of a bungee as Abby Gayle stretched it across the Murphy bed. "This is my friend Abby Gayle, and my name is Jix."

"Jenks?"

No. J-I-X. It's a long story…my mother gave me her maiden name. And your name is?"

"My friends call me Que. That too is a long story," he said, with an amusing gleam in his eye.

Soon he would be gone, and Jix knew little more than when she'd first seen him. He had recently moved to Springhill; he lived with a friend, but he didn't say if the friend was the same man they'd seen him talking to; he answered to Que. Not much to go on.

Calling the man Que was awkward, but Jix addressed him by name. "I buy and sell antiques. I'm especially interested in trunks…the small camelbacks, in particular." She reached inside the car, tore off a piece of the Hardee's sack, and jotted down her phone number. Handing the scrap of paper to their helper, she said, "I pay a finder's fee. If you know of anyone with trunks or old furniture, glassware, photo albums, books, vintage clothing…anything, really…for sale, give me a call. I pay ten percent of the purchase price to the finder. Call me. I'm always looking for things for resale."

He agreed he would contact her if he found anything of interest, said his good-byes amid many thanks for his help, and then walked down the alley and out of sight.

One final check of the massive bed resting like an Egyptian sarcophagus, and the girls were on their way home.

Chapter Twelve

Officer Bird sipped lemonade at a table in the food court located in Brookline Mall. She checked her watch against a clock suspended above the information booth. They had five minutes until the agreed upon meeting time—tardiness headed her list of pet peeves.

"Hi! So good of you to meet with us." Three women arrived in time to avoid a tongue lashing from Avonelle Bird about promptness, or more specifically, the lack thereof.

"We're not late, are we?" Jix looked at her watch.

"No, you're right on time," the policewoman, dressed in jeans and a floral print blouse, replied. It was her day off, and she had agreed to meet with Jix and Abby Gayle to share information on what they referred to as *the Bethany investigation.* She'd intended to go to the mall to return a purchase, so when Jix called to ask if they might meet, she'd agreed. And besides, the police lady found the trunk lady and her friend to be adventurous and likeable.

Margee smiled as Jix introduced her. "This is my mother Margee Fairmont. My daughter and granddaughter are riding the carousel. They'll join us as soon as Carol can convince Dinah there will be no more rides for today."

Pleasantries were exchanged as Abby Gayle took drink orders. Once the ladies were seated and sharing a double order of spring rolls from Saigon Sally's, Officer Bird noted information in her notebook as Jix and Abby recapped their encounter with Que and his elusive friend.

"We'll notify law enforcement there."

"Have you talked with Laura Riddling?" Abby Gayle asked Officer Bird.

"I've been to her house twice, but no one came to the door. Either she isn't home, or she's not answering."

Jix considered Richard Manikin's prediction of more current, pressing cases having priority. The lady cop's comment left an impression she would keep trying to contact the only known acquaintance of Bethany Perkins but not with a sense of urgency—at least not with the same measure of urgency that plagued Jix.

"We'll stay on it," Officer Bird assured the ladies. "Our main focus is finding the man who attempted to run over you two. Information he may be in the Springhill area is helpful."

The mall buzzed with Saturday morning shoppers and food court diners. A lengthy line of restless children waited their turn at an ornate lighted carousel. Serenaded by steady um-pa-pahs emanating from a calliope, little kids astride wild-eyed, wooden horses, glided up and down, up and down, round-and-round.

Abby Gayle spotted Carol holding Dinah, second in line for the next ride. She pointed them out to Jix who launched an arm-flailing attempt to get their attention. Finally, Dinah saw her grandmother and waved back.

Jix wanted to walk over and watch Dinah ride on the carousel, but she certainly didn't want to be rude to Officer Bird. After all, she'd agreed to meet on her day off.

Content to watch from afar, Jix was about to sit down when someone caught her eye. She grabbed Abby Gayle's arm.

"Look! Look who's in line at the Greek Gyro!" All eyes focused on the Greek eatery.

Bird was the first to reply, "That's Richard. Richard Manikin." She raised her hand to motion, but he was facing forward and couldn't see her.

"And in line in front of him is Laura Riddling," Jix noted.

Margee stood to see past the crowd. "No. That's Lucy Wessinger. I don't know her personally, but she's active in community theatre."

A puzzled Jix turned to Abby Gayle. "Doesn't she look like Mrs. Riddling? And she is in line with Richard."

Abby Gayle thought about the woman for a moment. "Her hair is different. Mrs. Riddling's hair is longer and held with a clip at the nape of her neck. This woman has shorter hair brushed back on the sides. Otherwise, she's a dead ringer for Laura Riddling."

Officer Bird solved the mystery, "It's Lucy Wessinger. She and Laura Riddling are twins."

This was news to Jix. "Twins! How do you know this?"

"I've known Richard for years and consider him a friend. I've purchased my last three cars from his dealership," she laughed. "Not long after his mother-in-law moved into the house across the street from him, she had a break in. We investigated and, at that time, I met Mrs. Riddling and her sister. They are identical twins."

"Do they live together?" Margee asked.

"I don't think so. But I only met Lucy once. I say we take advantage of this opportunity. Excuse me." Officer Bird dodged and elbowed her way through mall goers to where the owner of the town's largest car dealership had inched up to the counter to place his order. Lucy Wessinger stood by his side.

The three exchanged cordial greetings followed by an invitation for Richard and Lucy to join Officer Bird and the others. She returned to the table to find Margee and Carol had taken a tired, little Dinah home for a nap.

Once Lucy was introduced to Jix and Abby Gayle, those with a taste for gyros prepared to dig in. Avonelle Bird, Jix, and Abby Gayle finished the last of the spring rolls and considered ordering more; instead, they opted for something sweet, sending Abby Gayle to The Cookie Store. As Richard and Lucy finished their gyros, Jix expressed how glad she was to meet Mrs. Riddling's twin sister.

Richard wiped his lips with a paper napkin and smiled at the lady seated next to him. "Aunt Lucy is helping out at our house until Paula and the girls return from Italy. She keeps the animals and me well fed. And she helps Mom Riddling when she needs something. I'll be glad when Paula gets home, but I'll miss Aunt Lucy, too." She reached over and patted his arm.

"Where do you live? My mother said she knew you from your performances in community theatre."

As was true with her sister, Lucy Wessinger wore an ageless aura set in place by natural beauty. Although she and her sister had the same genetic makeup, it was apparent each had distinctive personalities. Bubbly, outgoing Lucy was the exact opposite of Laura whose dislike of change had tied her to the past.

"I live a few miles out of town. My husband Lester and our son Robert are pecan farmers. We have several acres of pecan groves." She seemed pleased. "I stay at Richard and Paula's during the day and go home at night...until she returns."

"We met your sister," Abby Gayle joined in.

"I've tried to contact her," Officer Bird injected. "Do you have a current phone number for her? The number I have is no longer in service."

Richard answered, "She's had the phone temporarily disconnected. I'm in the process of getting it reconnected. Mom Riddling likes her privacy," he chuckled.

Lucy added, "Laura is really a sweet person. She can be funny and charming although she is occasionally victim to what we refer to as *mood changes*. Nothing serious. She's set in her ways. You said you've met her. Being as she doesn't go out much, may I ask where you met?"

Again, Richard answered, "Mrs. Haynes visited her. She is restoring Aunt Amelia's trunk. I told you we'd decided to have it restored as a gift for Betty Sue."

"Yes, you did, dear. I'm anxious to see how it turns out." She turned to Jix, "Did you get the trunk unlocked?"

"A locksmith opened it. It is my understanding the key was misplaced years ago."

"Oh, there was never a key, as far as I know," Lucy folded her hands and leaned her elbows on the table.

"Seriously?" Jix could not contain her surprise. "Do you remember the trunk? Your sister Amelia owned it, right?"

"The trunk never belonged to Amelia. It came into her possession, and she kept it for years, but she didn't own it."

"Who did?" Abby Gayle asked.

"Bethany Perkins. After Bethany's disappearance, her mother was so distraught, she moved from her home in Mississippi. We heard from her once or twice at first but then lost touch completely after a few years. I remember first seeing the trunk at Amelia's..." she thought for a few seconds..."after Bethany had vanished. I don't know who gave it to Amelia. My guess would be Bethany's mother, before she moved away. But that is nothing more than an assumption. I don't know."

Officer Bird wrote in her notebook as fast as a court reporter. Richard leaned back, crossed his arms, and listened as if all this were news to him.

"Disappearance? Bethany disappeared?" Jix was shocked by this news.

"Oh my, it was so long ago. I'll have to think on this for a while." Lucy looked about. "The mall is becoming more crowded. It's so noisy I can hardly hear myself think." She addressed Richard, "Shall we meet later today or tomorrow afternoon? I need to regather my thoughts. These things took place so long ago. Laura is likely to remember more about Bethany than I, but I hesitate to ask for fear of upsetting her."

Richard answered, "Just think on these things, Aunt Lucy." To the others, he said, "Let's get together, say...tomorrow afternoon. You ladies come to my house around three. Should we ask Mom Riddling to join us?"

"I think not, dear. As I've said, Laura and Bethany Ann didn't get along." Turning to Jix, Lucy asked, "Was there anything in the trunk?"

72

"I have a list of items we found inside. I'll bring it," Abby Gayle volunteered.

"Splendid! And Officer Bird, I hope you'll join us." Lucy was delighted.

"Of course, I'll stop by, but I won't be able to stay long," she said. It had been three months since she'd last had a weekend off work. Even so, her curiosity was gaining momentum. She wanted to know what had happened to Bethany Ann Perkins.

Chapter Thirteen

After Richard and Lucy left, a trip to J. C. Penney's became the first stop on what turned out to be an afternoon shopping spree. Early summer sales offered bargains neither Abby Gayle nor Jix could resist. Exhausted and ready for supper, Jix dropped her sidekick off a little before six and then headed home.

"Hi," Margee greeted her daughter, laden with shopping bags she piled on the kitchen counter. "You two made it a day at the mall, didn't you?"

"It wasn't our original intention, but the sales were too good to miss." Jix pulled a blouse from a bag and held it up for Margee to see. "Look at this. Do you like it?"

"I love it. It would go well with my red, pleated skirt."

"That's what I thought; it's for you. You might like to wear it to Ramone's. I made reservations for dinner on your birthday."

"Oh! I love eating there. As you know, the prime rib is to die for. Thank you for thinking of me." She embraced Jix. "I'm going to try the blouse with the skirt...I'll be right back." She darted toward the bedroom but stopped when a thought flashed to mind that needed to be expressed before it faded away. "I almost forgot. Someone called. I took a message; it's on the pad by the phone. Oh, and I made a beef stew out of the leftover roast beef...we can eat anytime." And off she dashed.

Bill came in, opened the refrigerator, and leisurely surveyed the contents. "What are we having for supper?" He pulled the pop-top on a can of soda.

"Beef Stew. Where's Carol?"

"She and Dinah are eating with her friend Stephanie. They're taking the kids to a place called Chunky Cheese or something like that...for pizzas, I think." He held out his arms, and she slid into them.

He snuggled her neck and asked, "How was your day? I hesitate to ask for details; just say good or not so good."

She kissed him before answering, "You're silly. It was a good day. And yours?"

Before he could answer, Margee sashayed in with the savoir-faire of a high fashion model working the runway. "Voilà. What do you think?" She twirled around. Red shoes with rhinestone buckles matched her skirt and blouse to a tee.

"Beautiful!" Jix clapped her hands. "You look like you've stepped out of a fashion magazine."

"I feel like I've stepped out of a magazine. Let me change, and we'll eat. Did you see the phone message?"

"I got sidetracked."

She picked up the note pad to find her offer to the mysterious Mr. Que had paid off. "Yay! Terrific! This is the man who helped load the Murphy bed."

Bill stirred and sampled the stew. He took bowls from places set at the table and filled each. Margee returned and set cole slaw and rolls on the table.

"Honey, you and Mom go ahead and eat…this will only take a minute. I'll call from the phone in the den."

Consumed with curiosity, she dialed the number. When no one answered, she was about to hang up. Suddenly, "Hello," a man's voice resonated in her ear.

"Yes, hello. Is this Que? I am returning his call."

"Yes, it is. Is this Jenks? Sorry, Jix?"

"Yes. My mother said you called."

"Remember? You said to let you know if I found stuff you can resale. And you said you pay a finder's fee."

"What have you found?"

"Trunks, a canopy bed, a pie safe, and a few other things. This woman lives a little ways outside of Springhill. She hired me to hang a new door on a storage building. I saw all this old stuff piled up inside and asked her if she was thinking about selling any of it. Told her about you, and she said she'd be glad for you to come look, if you're interested."

"I am definitely interested. When is a good time to come?"

"Anytime. She doesn't go anywhere. I can meet you at the antique store where you got the bed…or the train station, whichever suits you."

"How about Monday morning? I have plans for tomorrow afternoon, but I can meet you around nine on Monday morning. Is that too early?"

"No. Nine is fine. It's a date. I'll be in the alley behind the antique store."

"Nine o'clock. Monday morning. I'll be there…and thanks."

She hung up and stared at her mother's note. Meeting with this man would throw her a day behind on trunk work. Que was a friend of the perpetrator of a hit and run; the more time she spent with him, the more likely she was to gain access to his friend.

Earl had missed several days due to a swollen knee; trunks were coming in faster than they were being completed. She would have to make up lost time by working at night.

Erring on the side of caution, Jix decided she would tell Officer Bird of her rendezvous with Que when they met at Richard's the following afternoon.

⊶

"I have another engagement, so I won't be able to stay long," Officer Bird explained, as she joined the gathering on the Manikin's patio. Jix and Abby Gayle had arrived early and were engaged in merry conversation with Richard and Lucy.

Once everyone had served themselves from a three-tiered plate of sweets, they found a place to sit.

Lucy said, "I've been thinking about the details of Bethany Ann's disappearance. It has been so long ago, I may not remember everything, but I'll tell you what I can recall. Now dear," she turned to Jix, "what do you want to know?"

"When did she disappear? Did she leave on her own, or were there suspicious circumstances?"

78

Richard poured a drink and settled on a chaise lounge padded with canvas-covered cushions. Avonelle Bird leaned back in a wicker rocker, her notebook in hand.

Gently swaying in an outdoor glider, Lucy mentally sorted Jix's queries before answering. "Bethany and Amelia were childhood friends. The two were more like sisters than Laura and me. They tagged along with us although most of the time, we would sneak off and try to leave them behind," she chuckled. "Amelia was the typical little sister pest. She was the baby of our family. Mother had her late in life; Laura and I were twelve when Amelia was born." She paused to take a sip of iced tea, then added, "There was a brother between us and Amelia who died. His name was Robert but we called him Bobby. I named my son after him."

"Bobby?" Jix leaned forward. "How old was he when he died?"

"Three."

"Oh. So sorry."

"Pneumonia. As I was saying, Bethany and Laura didn't get along. Things took a turn for the worse when the little girls were in high school...we referred to Amelia and Bethany as the little girls although neither was little. Both girls were tall and very athletic. Bethany played basketball, ran track, and pitched on a softball team. She could run like a rabbit."

Abby Gayle interrupted, "And yet, she writes in her diary she didn't swim. How strange."

Richard said, "Paula is afraid of water. Supposedly, her mother made her fearful by being overly protective. She doesn't swim but plays tennis. She likes to hike and do outdoorsy things. I don't find it strange Bethany wasn't a swimmer."

Bringing the glider to a standstill with the toe of her shoe, Lucy folded her arms and continued, "No, I suppose not. I've known a few people who don't swim. Anyway, by the time both Laura and I had married, she and Bethany had developed a fierce rivalry, mostly fueled by Laura. She accused Bethany of stealing, lying...I can't explain why. She never had proof, only constant accusations. Laura's always been easily offended, and the way she responds is often extreme. She's an unusually private person, to put it mildly."

Officer Bird spoke up, "Is your sister a widow?"

Lucy exchanged a knowing glance with Richard. "Oh no. Laura's husband is very much alive. Robert is a banker and lives in Mississippi with his," two fingers of each hand drew quotation marks in the air, "secretary."

"Robert?" Both Abby Gayle and Jix asked in unison.

"Another Robert. But she calls him Bobby," Richard said.

Officer Bird shook her head, "We gonna have to make a list to keep all these Bobbys straight."

Lucy was amused. "Do you have the diary?" she asked.

Avonelle Bird retrieved the book from her purse and handed it to Lucy. She thumbed through, unaware of the discovery concerning the coded message.

Jix pointed to the heart drawn on the front cover. "B.A.P. is Bethany Ann Perkins. Do you know what the R.V. Q stands for?'

"That can only be Bethany's boyfriend, Robert Vincent Quayling. They were sweet on each other from the fifth grade. Lovely boy, she called him Bobby. The Quaylings were pillars of the community. Bobby's father was a doctor, and his mother was the local librarian."

Officer Bird added another Bobby to her list.

Jix wondered if Lucy would ever tell of Bethany's disappearance, but she dared not be rude or seem overanxious. Approaching from a different angle, she asked, "When did Bethany disappear? The last entry in the diary is June of nineteen fifty-seven. Was it long after that?"

"I wouldn't want to assign an exact date to anything," she replied thoughtfully. "If memory serves me, there was a class picnic held in the park on the banks of Lake Claremont. Perry Seabacher, the chemistry teacher at the school, had a house on the lake. That day, he took small groups for a ride in his newly acquired speedboat as a special treat. Perry was proud as a peacock of that boat. Most of the students had never seen, much less ridden in, a boat that skimmed across the water at high speed. I don't know if I ever knew the details of what happened, but suffice it to say, the boat hit something in the water and capsized. Everyone was thrown overboard; none were wearing life vests. Bethany's body was never found, even though the lake was dragged more than once. All aboard were recovered, but one of the girls drowned. This happened so long ago. I know I've forgotten things that were common knowledge at the time."

"How very sad." All agreed with Abby Gayle.

"Mrs. Wessinger, do you recall someone named Bobby who also attended the picnic?" Jix asked.

"I wouldn't be surprised to find more than one Bobby or Robert in that graduating class. This was a popular boy's name at the time. There were an unusually large number of graduates, close to a hundred seniors that year. I remember because the graduation ceremony was held in the football stadium due to lack of room in the auditorium. And, of course, it rained earlier that day, and everything was wet or muddy." Signaling a pause with her index finger, she pointed to the sky, "I do remember a boy of Spanish descent named Roberto...they called him Rob...or Bob. And I know Bethany's boyfriend, Bobby, was there," she answered.

"Do you remember anyone named Roselyn? Was she in the class of '57?"

"Roselyn Redmond was the girl that drowned."

Chapter Fourteen

Abby Gayle gripped the steering wheel of her Suburban. Breakfast aromas of steak biscuits and strong, steaming coffee filled the car as they sped along asphalt.

"How many Bobbys do we have?" asked Jix. "Three?"

"Four," said the driver. "Laura and Lucy's brother, Lucy's son, Laura's husband, and Bethany's boyfriend. Four we know of."

"Let's hope that's all." Jix collected wrappers and Styrofoam cups to stuff in a sack. "We can eliminate Bobby, the little brother. And probably Lucy's son...he'd be too young to be involved in this."

"That leaves Bethany's boyfriend and Laura's husband. The husband would have been twelve, or more, years older than Bethany. Doesn't seem likely he would have attended a high school graduation party."

Racing against the clock, Abby Gayle maintained a steady speed to arrive on time for their appointment.

Cruising past the Springhill city limit sign, Jix verbally noted that which she considered to be of importance, "No matter what transpires today, we must not leave town without eating at the tearoom."

Arriving with minutes to spare, the Suburban dodged ruts in the poorly maintained alley. An older model pickup truck was parked near the loading ramp behind the antique store.

"Is that his vehicle?" asked Jix. "It could belong to someone in the antique store, I suppose."

Abby Gayle rolled to a stop beside the truck. Jix waved out the window to Que as he slid off the seat and approached the early morning visitors.

"Good day, ladies," he smiled.

"And a good morning to you." Jix reached out to shake his hand. "You remember my friend." She leaned back as Abby Gayle leaned forward to extend a greeting.

"Follow me. The lady is expecting us." He got back in the truck to lead the way.

A fifteen-minute drive from Springhill ended on the last leg of a dusty, country road that was little more than a trail located in the middle of nowhere. They parked near a primitive house that needed so many repairs, one would be challenged as to where to begin. To the dismay of meandering chickens, a pack of yard dogs on duty swarmed from underneath the porch to sound a threatening alarm.

Jix noted a large pond not far from the house. The surrounding woods were thick with undergrowth shaded by towering pines and sprawling oaks. In the distance, a sunbeam bounced off a tin roof atop an outhouse.

The screen door slammed behind a little woman with gray-streaked, dishwater-blonde hair clutching a straw broom by a shortened broomstick. She swung what was left of the worn-out thing while shouting commands to the dogs to shut up.

A tiny person—but only in stature—Beryl Sanford had a reputation of being one neither dog nor man would care to challenge. She was dressed in jeans so faded, only a hint of blue remained. In spite of rising temperatures, she wore a plaid, flannel shirt with the sleeves rolled up to her elbows.

"Y'all come on over to the storage building, and take a look." She stood the broom against the porch railing and clopped down the steps to lead the way to a shed on the far side of a one-car garage.

Abby Gayle held her breath when a stiff breeze circulated an odor that could only be coming from sour slop in a pig's trough.

"Watch out for chicken poop," the wiry little woman warned as they made their way to the wooden shed, which appeared to be somewhat sturdier than the main house. The chickens had moved away from dogs and visitors to another part of the grass-bare yard.

Widow Sanford unlocked the newly hung door. Que admired his handiwork as Jix and Abby Gayle stepped inside; then he followed. Footsteps on the rickety plank floor sent a mouse family scurrying through a hole created by a missing pine knot.

Unfazed by the sudden influx of visitors, the raccoon creeping along a rafter did not scurry but fixed an innocent, glassy-eyed stare on the intruders. Que stepped up to confront the masked creature.

85

"Step outside, ladies. Move away from the building until I can convince it to leave. Raccoons are sometimes rabid," he said.

Abby Gayle pleaded, "Don't hurt it. It's as scared of us as we are of it."

"I'm not scared of a raccoon, and I'm not going to hurt this one. Move slowly to the door." He kept his eye on the animal that had backed into a corner.

Once outside, Abby Gayle and Beryl Sanford decided to use the delay to look at quilts. They went inside the house and left Jix to wait outside in case Que needed assistance.

The only sounds Jix heard were those of a few birds conversing in the treetops or a chicken excited at the discovery of an unsuspecting insect. A check on the whereabouts of the dogs found them sprawled in the dirt near the porch steps.

A tire swing hung from a low branch on a magnolia tree; a claw foot bathtub filled with flowering plants anchored a birdhouse atop an iron pipe pole. A larger than average black and white cat, stretched across the porch railing, followed Jix's every move through half-closed eyes.

The woods surrounding the house were a jungle of overgrown honeysuckle vines and patches of kudzu, so much so, she almost missed it.

Had it not been for the sun's reflection in the side mirror of the black sedan, Jix would have never seen the car camouflaged by head-high weeds and kudzu clinging to the remains of an abandoned hay baler.

She looked away in case there was someone in the car. While Que evicted the raccoon, she formulated a plan.

Abby Gayle soon returned in the company of a happy quilt salesperson. As soon as the raccoon was relocated, the women resumed their exploration of items in the storage shed.

Jix dickered with the old lady over two trunks. One trunk in particular was of interest, being as Jix recognized it as a Union officer's campaign trunk in surprisingly good condition for its age. However, Beryl's asking price was too high.

"I can't pay that much, Mrs. Sanford. I have to buy so I have room to make a little when I resale. And take into account, I will have money in the restoration." She thought for a moment before presenting a tried and true ploy. "I'll make you an offer on both trunks and the pie safe. This is the best I can do." She offered a lump sum that sounded tempting to a seller who had no need for the items but could use the money.

Sold! The seller was thrilled, the buyer predicted a profit potential, and the finder mentally tallied a fifty-dollar reward.

Abby Gayle bought an old, wooden, medicine cabinet that had a cracked, hazy mirror and was missing a knob. She knew if she couldn't find a place for it, Jix would put it in her booth at the antique mall and sell it.

Chapter Fifteen

Employing the trial and error method—aided by Que's muscular power—Jix and Abby fit the trunks and pie safe into the Suburban.

"Y'all are welcome to come in and wash up. Those trunks are nasty. Been sitting out there for years, and before that they were in the barn," Beryl said.

"If you don't mind, I need to visit your facilities before we get on the road." Jix turned to Abby Gayle, "I suggest we both go. We have a long ride ahead."

Abby Gayle picked up on Jix's suggestive tone. "I think you're right," she agreed.

"Y'all come inside and wash up first. The outhouse is at the end of the trail out back."

"Lead the way." Jix and the others followed their hostess inside.

89

Que commented to Abby Gayle as they climbed the porch stairs, "I'm impressed with how much we were able to pack in your SUV."

"It is handy. I only bother with the trailer if I am hauling something the size of the Murphy bed. I used to drive a long-bed pickup like your truck." Abby Gayle stepped inside when he held the screen door open.

"Don't you be giving away my truck," Beryl joked.

Que chuckled. "I borrowed Miss Sanford's truck to meet you."

"How'd you get here?" asked Jix, although she already knew.

"A friend dropped me off and will pick me up. As a matter of fact, I need to hurry up." He glanced at his watch.

⚬─

The house was spotlessly clean. In the roomy kitchen, lace-trimmed, red-checkered curtains brightened a window over a sink with no need for faucets—a hand pump easily accessed cold, clear, well water. Ladder-back chairs painted white fenced a round, oak table.

Jix and Abby Gayle excused themselves to follow Beryl's directions to the detached latrine. Once out of earshot, Jix told Abby Gayle of the car parked not far from the house, near the pond.

"What are we going to do? We know the man is dangerous. I don't think we should approach him again," Abby Gayle said.

Jix presented a possibility, "Que could have driven the car here. If so, there's nobody in it."

"He said a friend dropped him off and would come to get him."

"Yes, he did say that. Here's what I think; if we try to follow the two of them, we may lose them. If the man we encountered is on the premises, I say, let's not let him get away," said Jix.

"That's all fine and dandy, except we need a plan this time...preferably a plan that works in our favor. And don't forget about Que. Confucius say woman should never deal with more than one man at a time."

"I'll get Beryl alone and explain the situation to her. Either she'll help, or she won't. It won't hurt to ask."

Jix turned to go back inside. Her only face-to-face encounter with the driver of the car flashed on her memory board. "I must admit, I question the wisdom of confronting this person again."

"You think? Beryl is as old as the hills! She'll be no help whatsoever! We should let them leave and follow them. This is crazy, Jix! We can't subdue two men. We weren't successful at stopping one." Abby Gayle sought to reason with her friend. "Here's a sober thought. Let's call the police. Officer Bird has surely contacted them to look for the car. We simply call and tell them where it is."

The back door slammed, sending a teetering pot tumbling over the porch railing and frightening two kittens asleep in a washtub. Beryl appeared with her hands propped on her hips, "Y'all find the privy?"

Jix walked over and whispered, "Where's Que?"

"He's on the front porch. I need to get some floorboards replaced before I fall through and break my neck. He's going to give me an estimate of what he would charge to do the work. Why?"

91

Jix said to Abby Gayle, "Keep him occupied while I tell Beryl what's going on." Abby Gayle headed around the house to the front porch.

Beryl asked, "What *is* going on?"

Jix gave a breviloquent recap of her previous dealings with Que and his friend.

When asked whether Beryl thought they should call the police, follow the men, or do nothing at all, she replied, "Here's what we're going to do."

Chapter Sixteen

"My boys, Ralph and Randale, live on the other side of that catfish pond." She pointed over Jix's head. "You be certain Que stays busy, and I'll give my boys a call." As Jix walked away to join Abby Gayle, Beryl merrily muttered, "Let the games begin."

Within minutes, a big, black, truck with over-sized tires, a gutted muffler, and a dust cloud riding its bumper rolled to a stop a few feet in front of the bathtub filled with blooming flowers. A man who made a linebacker look like a dwarf slid off the front seat in a hurry, leaving the door wide open. Ralph had arrived.

"Hey, Mama," he grinned at his mother.

"Hey there, darlin'. You doin' all right?"

"Yes, ma'am." He positioned himself near Que. "Y'all walk with me over to the pond. I got something I want to show you."

Que's eyes widened, and his jaw dropped. He swallowed hard but didn't utter a word.

"We'll take the trail through the back yard. You go first." Ralph stepped behind Que and gestured for his mother to be next in line. Jix and Abby Gayle followed as the procession proceeded down the porch steps.

The dogs sprang into action. Two pups ran ahead, barking as if they'd picked up the scent of a rabbit; three older dogs closed ranks behind Abby Gayle. The cat casually observed from the porch railing.

Down the trail, past the outhouse, and on toward the pond, the five trekked. They reached their destination when they came upon Randale—a duplicate of his brother—leaning against the fender of the black car. He aimed a shotgun at a tall, thin man with his hands stretched high above a red baseball cap.

"Hey, Mama," Randale Sanford smiled at his mother.

"Hey there, darlin'. You doin' all right?"

"Sure am. I believe you've got a trespasser on your land."

"He's more than a trespasser. The law's looking for him." Beryl instructed Jix to tell her boys how she knew the two men.

Jix repeated the story she'd shared with Beryl, emphasizing how Abby Gayle had suffered with bruises, aches, and pains.

Randale narrowed his eyes. "What do you have to say for yourself?" he asked his captive.

The fidgety man, who'd not given his name, looked away and refused to reply. Que watched, painfully aware he could be of no help to his friend.

Ralph was about to say they should return to his mother's house and contact the police when, instead, he suddenly began to dance around, stomping his feet and yelling.

"Ants!" he screamed. "I'm standing in a fire ant bed!" In a flash, zillions of the red insects rushed to the surface to protect their nest.

The big man stomped his feet harder, jerked his pants legs up as far as they would go, and wildly brushed his painfully burning, welted legs. An army of ants covered his boots and socks.

Ralph distanced himself from the ant bed and fell on the ground, all the while beating insects off his legs. Beryl and Jix rushed to unlace his boots and pull them off. Abby Gayle quickly discovered no matter how hard she shook his socks, the pesky creatures appeared to be unfazed.

The dogs began to jump and bark, adding to the commotion generated by Ralph's discomfort and Beryl's attempts to comfort her son.

Making matters worse, two young hounds launched into a dogfight, sending Jix and Abby Gayle scrambling to get out of the way.

Randale kicked and screamed at the dogs. He tried to grab the redbone hound by its collar with one hand while holding the gun on his captive with the other. Pandemonium peaked when the other dogs joined the ruckus.

Only Que noticed when the driver of the black sedan sprinted toward the pond, calling for Que to run too.

Abby, Jix, and Randale chased after the escapees; the sedan driver was far ahead of Que. Adding to the craziness, the dogs stopped fighting and joined the chase.

The red cap sailed off the man's head as his feet slapped the ground. He zigzagged toward a wooded area only to be redirected by the barking dogs toward the catfish pond.

Gasping for breath at the water's edge, the runner spotted a rowboat tethered to a post. With no time to wait for Que and no other route of escape, he untied the boat, pushed off, and paddled with one oar.

Randale took aim at the boat and with one shot blasted a hole in it. Pond water gushed through the opening, flooding the vessel and arousing cries for help.

"I can't swim! Help me! I can't swim!" Standing on the seat of the sinking craft, the man flapped his arms and persistently shouted for help.

Ralph burst on the scene, dashing past the others who were about to enter the pond. "I'll get him!" shouted the big man, seizing the opportunity to rid himself of any remaining ants and save the man at the same time. Barefoot, Ralph dove in and swam to the partially submerged boat.

Anxiously watching the rescue effort, Randale also kept an eye on Que. The dogs had lost interest in the fracas and thirstily lapped up pond water.

Que's remark was almost lost in the commotion.

Jix spun on her heels, grabbed his arm, and screamed, "What did you say?"

He snatched his arm away and clamped his lips tight.

She screamed at Que again, "What did you say?"

When he didn't answer, she grabbed him by his shoulders, dug her fingernails into his flesh, and shook him. "I want to hear you say it again. Tell me what you said!"

Que bowed his head and sadly repeated unguarded words spoken in the heat of the moment, "Thank God she's safe. She can't swim."

Chapter Seventeen

Unable to stop trembling, the wet runaway slumped beside Que on the front seat of the black car. He had retrieved a towel from the back seat where all their worldly belongings were stored.

Ralph walked his mother and the dogs back to the house; Randale stood beside the car with shotgun in hand.

Jix squatted down to eye-level with the person sitting in the driver's seat.

"Bethany?"

Que stroked his companion's shoulders. "Give us a moment." He shook his head, "Please, give us a moment."

Abby Gayle stood beside Jix. "There's no hurry. You have a lot to tell, and we are anxious to hear," she said.

Everyone waited...for what? No one knew for sure.

And then the first words spoken by one resurrected from the past shattered the silence.

"What now?" the woman asked.

Jix replied, "There is no need for you to run or hide anymore. We have to report this to the police in Brookline, so they will call off the hunt for you. There is a warrant for your arrest."

Abby Gayle blurted, "You could have killed us! You nearly did! Why? Why would you?" Jix reached over and patted her friend's hand. All of this had come to a head, and overwrought emotions were at a breaking point.

Jix turned to face Randale. "Let's go to your mother's house and decide what to do next." He responded in agreement.

Que asked, "May Bethany get dry clothes to change into?" He glanced in the back seat. It was then Jix realized they were living in the car.

"Sure," she said. "Get what you need. We'll walk back to the house, and you can tell us why you've been missing for thirty years." As a measure of caution, she added, "Give me your car keys."

⊶

Jix called Officer Bird to report Bethany Ann Perkins as alive and well and sitting in Beryl Sanford's parlor.

The policewoman made plans to go through proper channels to take the hit and run driver into custody. A few hours earlier on that same day, Jix Haynes would have rejoiced over the prospects of the driver going to jail. But things had changed.

The driver was a person for whom Jix had acquired an undeniable affinity. The young girl of Jix's imagination had materialized into a tangible, mature woman. The issue was no longer about an irresponsible driver—not since it had become clear the driver was Bethany. When it came to incarcerating Bethany Ann Perkins, Jix wanted no part. Without reservation, she was willing to drop the charges.

Abby Gayle was not so willing. Regardless of the mental state of the driver or bizarre circumstances which may have led to her impulsive behavior, she felt the woman should be held accountable for what could have caused serious injury—even death.

Both argued their point; neither would concede.

Abby Gayle suggested they confront Bethany and let her decide whether she should be held accountable or not.

The two women approached the anomalous couple seated on Beryl's living room sofa. Ralph leaned against the doorframe, and Randale straddled a kitchen chair turned backwards. Beryl had gone to the kitchen.

"Why did you endanger our lives? You could have killed us both had we not gotten out of your way," Abby Gayle demanded an answer.

Looking worse for the wear, Bethany remained silent.

Que answered, "Bethany wouldn't deliberately hurt a fly. She panicked. Try to understand. She has run for so long, to flee is all she knows.

Beryl, who'd been listening from the adjoining room, came to the kitchen door. Changing the subject, she asked, "Who are you? Is Que your real name?"

The thin, beleaguered woman with wet hair and red, swollen eyes held the hand of the man sitting next to her. She looked at him adoringly. "This is my husband, Bobby Quayling."

Jix's knees weakened. She eased into a chair and dug her nails into the padded arms, holding on to steady her nerves. Bethany from a bygone era had risen from the pages of a diary like a Dickens' ghost to become flesh and blood. And now Jix discovered the initials on the cover of a book were those of a man she had befriended and grown to like.

Bethany continued, "His nickname is Que. He has done nothing other than stand by me. He's loved and protected me for thirty-two years." Bethany wiped her eyes with Que's bandana she'd used as a handkerchief.

Que defended his wife. "Look, you don't know the constant danger threatening Bethany. She hides to save her life." He heaved an exasperated sigh. "Our lives are complicated. A certain person with ill intent is looking for her. If she is arrested, she will be a sitting duck. She will be in imminent danger."

"He won't harm me himself. He has people do his dirty work." Before she buried her face in her hands to hide a flood of tears, Bethany atoned for her irrational behavior. "I am so sorry I caused you injury. All I could think of was getting away. Please forgive me."

Abby Gayle exclaimed, "Oh, all right! Jix, call Officer Bird and tell her we'll drop all charges. Ask what she recommends we do next."

Bethany raised her head and dabbed her eyes. "Let us go. We'll be on our way, and you'll never see us again."

Jix shook her head. "On your way to where? Is this how you want to spend the rest of your lives?"

Bethany answered, "You don't understand. As Que said, our situation is very complicated. If there were a simple solution, we would have found it by now. My life is not worth a plug nickel if a certain someone finds me. The only way for me to stay alive is to stay one step ahead of him."

Ralph asked, "Who is this person? Randale and I have friends in low places. We can get a message to this man he'll understand." Randale nodded that he was willing and ready to help.

Mama bear dashed into the room to protect her cubs. "Whoa! Hold on just a dadgum minute!" She shook her finger at Ralph first, then Randale. "You two have families to take care of. You need to stay out of this. Jix, call your cop friend. This is business for the law, not for my boys," she emphatically stated, in a tone none misunderstood nor dared to challenge.

Chapter Eighteen

"Bethany, Que, this is Officer Bird." Jix stood to greet the policewoman as she entered a small interview room on the third floor of the Brookline City Complex where police headquarters were housed.

Avonelle Bird, a small satchel tucked under her arm, acknowledged the introductions with, "Glad to meet you." She turned to a young man at her side, "This is detective Joe Martino. And due to my recent promotion and reassignment to the Brookline Criminal Investigation Unit, I am now Detective Bird."

Thumbs up accompanied congratulations. The two sat down at a rectangular table across from the Quaylings. Jix and Abby Gayle took a seat in metal, folding chairs pushed against the wall.

Detective Bird tallied a first impression of the thin, tall woman with dark, closely cropped hair. She then smiled at the companion, a solemn man who did not smile back. Each waited for someone else to speak.

Finally, Detective Bird broke the silence. "How are you folks doing this morning?" She greeted Bethany, whose expression suggested she was rapidly approaching her stress tolerance level.

Que answered, "We're doing the best we can. And you?"

"I'm good. Where'd you stay last night?" The detective continued.

Jix volunteered, "As you suggested, they came home with me. Que rode from Springhill with Abby Gayle, and I drove Bethany in her car."

Bird directed her remarks to Bethany. "A question has arisen concerning the possibility of foul play due to remarks recorded in a diary. Is this your diary?" The detective slid the book across the table.

The pale woman appeared to grow paler as she stared at the book. "May I?" she asked.

"Certainly."

Spellbound, Bethany held the diary as gently as holding a newborn.

Detective Martino repeated, "Is this your diary?"

"Yes, it is." Bethany turned the key and released the lock. "It has been stored in my trunk for many years." Memories fluttered from the pages like a kaleidoscope of butterflies when she looked inside. She closed the cover and took a deep breath.

Avonelle Bird propped her elbows on the table, leaned forward, and lowered her voice, "Mrs. Quayling, I want to help you…if you need help. But you have to be honest and tell me what is going on. Start back at the beginning, and tell me if you've witnessed a crime—if someone has threatened you. You're safe now; I can offer protection. But you have to tell all before I can help you."

Que reached for his wife's hand. He looked deep into her eyes in an attempt to reason with her. "Sweetheart, we have to stop running. The only way to change our situation is to face the enemy, and with help, we can make positive changes. So far, it has been the two of us, but this is an opportunity to right a wrong and stop this madness." He finger-brushed a stray strand of hair from her forehead. "Please listen. It's time to face the truth."

Bethany opened the diary again and scanned the pages as she spoke. "I suppose you're right." She swallowed a sob. He scooted his chair closer and put his arm around her shoulder.

Detective Bird offered words of reassurance, "I'm here to help in any way I can. Take your time. Start with the comments in the diary. Did you witness a murder?"

Acceptance of the inevitable overcame hesitation as Bethany launched into her tale. Words tumbled from her mouth to the ears of attentive listeners.

"I witnessed a murder. Although it took place years ago, I have a vivid recollection of every detail as if it happened yesterday. I have relived the scene thousands of times. I saw Bobby drown Roselyn the day of our graduation picnic." Her shoulders sagged as decades of pent-up emotions began to leak.

The detectives waited. Bobby "Que" Quayling held her hand, his head bowed as if in prayer while Jix and Abby Gayle maintained a statuesque stillness.

"There was a boating accident. Our chemistry teacher, Mr. Seabacher, had purchased a new speedboat, and throughout the afternoon, he took five passengers at a time out on the lake. Mr. Seabacher was enjoying showing off his boat. And the kids were having fun. He insisted Roselyn and I go despite our reluctance. We didn't want to hurt his feelings, so we agreed. We were so young and didn't know how to say no. We'd been taught to be respectful and polite to our elders. Also, we were both distressed about a dreadful predicament Roselyn had gotten herself into. She was upset about a spat she'd had earlier with Bobby. I don't swim, so we had no business allowing ourselves to be talked into doing something neither of us wanted to do. If only we'd been strong enough to refuse to go, she would be alive today." Bethany choked back a sob.

Everyone remained silent. She continued, "You see, Roselyn had told Amelia and me what had taken place earlier that day. The three of us were very close friends, more like sisters than friends." Her husband sensed her anguish and squeezed her hand.

She reached for a tissue to wipe her eyes then laced her fingers in her lap. "I should explain events that occurred prior to the class picnic."

"Take all the time you need," Detective Bird said.

"There's so much to tell, I find my thoughts are all over the place. I've spent endless hours reliving that horrible day. I've lost countless hours of sleep, but I have not talked about it."

"Can I get you a drink?" The detective asked.

"No, thank you, I'm fine. I need to go back to a few weeks before the picnic. Unfortunately, Roselyn had gotten involved with an older man. I had unintentionally walked in on them in an embrace. They acted as if they'd done nothing inappropriate. I pretended I thought nothing of it, but later when I confronted her, Roselyn admitted she was deeply involved.

Detective Martino said, "When you say 'involved', do you mean intimately?"

106

"Yes. Roselyn was pregnant, but she had not told him until the day of the picnic. In fact, she'd told him not long before our boat ride. He had ridden earlier, but when we felt obligated to appease Mr. Seabacher, Bobby said he wanted to go again. Roselyn was uncomfortable because of his reaction when she'd told him she was having his baby. He was angry, and that frightened her. When she found out he was going too, she asked Que to join us."

Jix moved to a chair closer to the table. "Excuse me. I'm wondering who Bobby is. I assume your husband is not the Bobby you are referring to."

"No, of course not. My Bobby was there, but this Bobby was a chaperone, along with his wife. They often chaperoned school events."

Detective Bird asked, "What was Bobby's last name?"

"Is his last name...not was," Bethany said.

"Is?"

"He is alive and well today. And he knows I saw him hold Roselyn under the water, and he will not stop searching until he finds me. Life jackets were available, but Bobby wouldn't let us wear one. He teased us about being childish. He kicked the life vests under the seats. Somehow Que managed to grab a vest and fling it in the water when the boat collided with debris. It was a miracle that I was able to latch onto it."

"And this Bobby...his last name is...?"

"Riddling. Bobby Riddling."

Chapter Nineteen

"So let me get this straight. Richard's father-in-law has been threatening the Quaylings all these years?" Bill Haynes sat on the side of the bed waiting for his wife to come out of the bathroom.

"Thas wha' she said." Jix appeared in the doorway gripping a foamy toothbrush with her teeth.

"How long are they staying with us? Do they have police protection?'

Jix disappeared. He listened for the water to stop running and watched for her to appear in the doorway. As she shuffled to her side of the bed, he passed her on his way to the bathroom.

"We don't have room for extra people long term." Jix sat down on the bed and slipped off her fuzzy slippers.

After David Fairmont died, Margee and Jix hired a contractor to turn an enclosed porch into a bedroom flooded with natural light. An additional bath and a cozy sitting room completed a part of the house Margee called home. To accommodate Bethany and Que, she had graciously moved into the nursery with Dinah, insisting the daybed near the baby's crib was comfortable enough for as long as their guests needed to stay.

Jix spoke to her husband in the adjoining room, "Austin invited them to ride along on his next haul to Texas. Abby Gayle has offered temporary housing. Detective Bird is also working on arrangements for a safe place for them to stay while she investigates Bethany's accusations. And, are you ready for this?"

He returned, slid between the sheets, and stretched out. Punching his pillow to get the right fit, he muttered, "Prob'ly not."

"Bethany suspects Amelia's death was also a homicide. Of all unlikely things, bees killed the woman. Bethany says her friend was allergic to insect stings, especially bees. The neighbor kept beehives, but Amelia stayed clear of them. The police are still investigating circumstances surrounding the incident. Detective Bird is working with a detective assigned to the case in Jackson where Robert Riddling lives with his young girlfriend."

"Sounds like something out of a mystery novel." Bill turned off the lamp on his side and pulled the cover up around his shoulders.

"You don't know the half of it," she stared through the darkness.

"But I'm going to, aren't I?"

Jix wiggled into a comfortable position. "Well, one thing is for sure; Bethany is terrified of Bobby Riddling. I don't know if she has reason to be or if she has worked herself into a state of paranoia. She tells of a boating accident on the day of the graduating class' picnic. I don't know if it was ever determined what caused the accident, but that's beside the point. Bethany doesn't swim and would have drowned, but she was able to grab a floating life preserver."

"Was Que on the boat?"

"Yes, he was in the water looking for Bethany and helping the teacher who was severely injured."

Jix paused as she recalled Bethany's account of the day's events. She told Bill how Bobby Riddling had tried to save Roselyn although she could swim. And how during all the confusion, Bethany saw him hold Roselyn under the water.

"If life vests were available, why wasn't Bethany wearing one?"

"According to her, Bobby Riddling wouldn't allow it. He teased them about being brave. If he intended to drown Roselyn, a flotation device would have made it difficult, and as I've already pointed out several times, she was an excellent swimmer. If Roselyn was dubious and wanted to wear a floatation device, it may have been because of the speedboat. Few women find speeding in anything fun or enjoyable...that's a guy thing."

"How could he have intended to drown her if the opportunity rested on a boating mishap?"

She speculated. "It doesn't seem likely he would have known there would be a collision. Had he known, you have to question whether he would have risked being injured. Could have been his lucky day, and the crash played into his plans to kill Roselyn. Bethany said Roselyn had told Bobby Riddling she was pregnant. Maybe the drowning wasn't premeditated; he snapped, and when the opportunity presented itself, Riddling took advantage."

"I suppose anything is possible." Bill didn't have an opinion as to the truth.

"Bobby Riddling drowned his pregnant girlfriend then realized Bethany, clinging to the life preserver, had seen him hold her under water."

"Only she witnessed this? Weren't there other people around?"

Jix explained the boat had traveled away from the picnic goers. Of the six people on the excursion, all were struggling, and the damaged craft was taking on water.

"And it doesn't take long to drown someone...I don't think. Based on past behavior, this man was known to be incorrigible. According to Bethany, he had a reputation of being self-absorbed," Jix said.

Bill didn't comment. He knew his wife was incapable of telling only part of a story. He rested quietly until she resumed.

"Bethany and Que were frightened of Bobby Riddling then, and they still are today. They presumed he would deny Bethany's account of what happened; they were kids, and he was an established businessman in their town."

"What did they do?"

"The way I understand it, Bethany made it to shore, and afterward, she and Que left town as quickly as possible. They considered telling the police, but they panicked and ran. Fear is a powerful motivator."

"And they've been on the run ever since?" he asked.

"Bobby Riddling was suspicious when Bethany's body was never recovered, and Que had left town. He hired detectives who quickly discovered an indisputable paper trail created when a Justice of the Peace married Bethany and Que. Discovering those records began a very long chase," Jix said.

"Why did they come here? Did they know Laura Riddling lives here?"

112

"Oh, yes. They came to this area because of Amelia's death and Paula inheriting the trunk. Bethany had given her close friend the trunk for safekeeping. She'd confided in Amelia about what she had witnessed and told her if anything ever happened to her...Bethany, not Amelia...Amelia should present the diary as evidence of what she, Bethany, had witnessed."

Jix rested while the flood of information washed over Bill. "I assume Amelia knew the confession was coded?" he asked.

"She did. To protect the diary, she never opened the trunk. Bethany was her bosom buddy, and she knew what Bobby Riddling was capable of. I still can't figure why Amelia stipulated that upon her death the trunk was to go to Paula."

"So what now? Anybody have a plan?" Despite this tantalizing tale, Bill's eyelids had grown heavy.

Jix answered, "Detective Bird's objective is to do whatever it takes to put Bobby Riddling behind bars. He may be responsible for Amelia's death too, albeit, that remains to be seen. But for now, the Quayling's safety is top priority. Abby Gayle offered to take them in until more permanent arrangements are made, and their car is stored in her garage. Everything has happened so fast. This morning we went to police headquarters; tonight I am trying to make sense out of what has happened and what needs to happen next."

"There's that cabin on Doe Ridge."

"What?"

"Remember? I told you we foreclosed on a log house atop Doe Ridge. There are six houses along the mountain range; only two are occupied year-round. The Quaylings could move there as caretakers until the police can make other arrangements or we sell the house, whichever comes first. I may be able to arrange a small salary for babysitting the property. Don't count on it, but I can see what I can arrange."

"Isn't there only one road to the mountaintop? Is there electricity up there?"

"Yes," he answered. "A state senator owned a summer home on the ridge a decade or so ago. He waved his magic wand, and electricity and phones appeared. Without his influence, I doubt there would be any sign of civilization up there. The road is impassable in winter; only hermits and hunters are drawn to the area...other than the senator. Far as I know, he was neither. I predict it will be a while before our foreclosure sells."

"That would be perfect, Bill. Better than perfect! They would be safe while we work on the case."

His eyes flew open. "We? No, no, not we. Not me. Certainly not me! I'm not working on a case," he stuttered.

Jix ignored him. "I'll call Detective Bird first thing in the morning. We'll talk with Bethany and Que at breakfast. Bobby Riddling is about to get a dose of his own medicine."

"Lord help us," Bill turned toward the wall and squeezed his eyes shut tight.

Chapter Twenty

Bouncing about in a four-wheel drive vehicle along a narrow, unpaved road with craters for potholes gave Leon Sopakco an opportunity to become acquainted with his most recent charges, Bethany and Bobby Quayling.

Sopakco, a twice-demoted detective, presently held the rank of officer. Protecting the couple was his first assignment since being transferred to the Brookline Criminal Investigations Unit. The cantankerous cop with bunions on the sides of his big toes hoped this was his last assignment before his retirement in three months.

Finding the cabin at the ridge crest was like finding the proverbial needle in a haystack. Sopakco, at the wheel, explored several trails branching off the main road, only to end up at a dead end or a hunter's abandoned blind. At last they lucked upon a trail leading to a building that looked more like a mountain lodge than a log cabin. What had been referred to as a cabin was, in fact, a spacious, well maintained, three-bedroom house constructed of logs. A front porch spanned the length of the house, complete with rocking chairs and water-deprived ferns shriveled in hanging baskets. Sopakco pulled along side the house and parked near the back, out of sight.

The mountain top oasis hugged a cliff. Where one would expect a back yard, there was instead a back porch sitting on the edge of a deep canyon with a panoramic view stretching as far as the eye could see.

The house was furnished with comfy, slipcovered chairs and sofas, reclaimed wood tables, soft pillows, bentwood rockers, and pops of color on painted accent pieces. Bethany looked in every room, delighted by the hominess of the place.

"Look at this fireplace." They eyed stone stacked from the hardwood floors to the exposed beams. A rough-hewn timber mantle bridged the width of the fireplace. "It looks like a real home, doesn't it?" Bethany said to her husband as he embraced her.

They heard Sopakco checking the window locks and closing the blinds. He had explored outside and made a mental note to trim overgrown shrubbery. When he talked to Detective Bird, he would ask her to send hedge clippers.

The men unloaded groceries and supplies. Bethany stocked the pantry and set aside canned tuna for lunch. For the first time in a long time, Bethany and Que dared to hope for happier days.

⌐⊸

A helper who was no help had put Jix further behind on trunk work. Earl had recruited his brother Jimmy to take his place while he recuperated from knee surgery.

Although a likeable fellow, working with power tools was not his forte. Jimmy paled at the mere sight of a circular saw; a triggered drill or a spinning sander unnerved the young man; and he held his breath to keep from breathing dust and paint stripper fumes, even when he wore a respirator. Everything he'd worked on had to be redone.

When the useless helper pinched his hand closing the heavy lid of a large trunk, Jix was relieved she wouldn't have to fire Earl's brother although she was sorry he had injured his hand. One problem was solved but another created. She had an idea for a temporary fix, contingent upon Detective Bird's approval. She phoned the lady cop.

"Hello. This is Jix Haynes. May I speak with Detective Bird?"

After a short wait, Avonelle Bird answered the phone. "Hello, Jix, I'm glad you called. I need to talk to you, but first, is there a problem with the Quaylings?"

Jix explained the situation with Earl and Jimmy and asked if she might offer the job to Que. Bird replied she would see if she could arrange transportation and protection.

Before the detective hung up, Jix asked, "Do you know anything more about the circumstances of Amelia's death?"

"Yes, I was going to call you, but I have been swamped with work. I've talked with authorities in Mississippi. Cause of death was anaphylactic shock apparently brought on by bee venom. The incident is under investigation due to suspicious circumstances. That's about all I can tell you." She excused herself and hurried on her way.

Disappointed this was not news, being as Bethany had known as much, Jix plopped down in a chair.

Lost in thought, she stared aimlessly at rows of leather trunk handles hanging on a pegboard. Bethany had said Amelia was allergic to bee stings and her neighbor kept beehives. Were those the bees Bethany encountered? If so, why would she risk going near the neighbor's hives?

Jix dialed Abby Gayle's number and waited.

"Hello."

"Hey. I'm going to Lucy Wessinger's pecan farm. Want to go?"

"Isn't Lucy at Paula's helping out while she's gone?"

"You're right. Let's go to Paula's. If Lucy's car is there, we'll pay her an unexpected visit. If not, we'll go to her farm."

"What's up, Sherlock? Why the sudden need to talk to Lucy?"

"My gut tells me that woman knows a lot more than she's told us," Jix said.

"Oh. Okay, I'll be ready by the time you get here."

Chapter Twenty-One

Jix parked beside Lucy's car and then entered the back yard through a wooden gate. The uninvited visitors stepped over a long garden hose stretching from the patio to the pool and made their way to the back door where a yellow cat waited patiently on the doormat.

Before Jix could ring the bell, Abby Gayle stopped her. "Wait," she whispered. "Let's see if she's busy. It's the least we can do being as we didn't call ahead." She tiptoed to the kitchen window and peered through a lower pane.

"Look! There she is. She's crying."

Jix moved to the window to see Lucy sitting at a breakfast banquette, her head buried in her hands. "I don't think she's crying. Looks like she's resting."

"The decent thing to do would be to go and let her have her privacy," Abby Gayle said.

Quietly leaving was no longer an option when Jix turned and stepped on the curious cat. The startled animal yowled in pain, scaled the fence, and disappeared.

119

Lucy rushed to the door to investigate the commotion. Her eyes were red but not from crying. She appeared to be someone who'd not slept soundly.

Once profound apologizes were offered for coming without calling, the ladies followed Lucy inside. She graciously set out three cups and offered tea or coffee. Jix, who'd volunteered to help, followed Lucy's instructions to put four cinnamon buns from the freezer into the microwave. When Jix asked about Lucy's husband and her son Robert, she was glad to talk about her loved ones.

Small talk and sugary-iced rolls brightened the morning. Lucy shared comical news of Paula and the girls' ill-fated adventure. They had taken the wrong bus and ended up in a remote Italian village where they'd waited overnight to get a bus back to civilization.

The three women predicted that Paula, lost in a foreign country and responsible for five lovely daughters, had yet to see the humor in her annoying plight. But they found the story amusing; especially the part where two women boarded the ancient bus carrying squealing piglets.

They shared the last cinnamon roll before—without warning—Lucy's mood soured. The frivolity of the moment could not bear the weight of her concern. Jix reached across the table and put her hand over Lucy's.

"What's the matter? You seem sad. We're good listeners. Rest assured anything you share would not leave this room."

Abby Gayle added, "Talking about whatever troubles you may ease your burden."

Lucy paused to consider how much she would share with the ladies, "I really can't talk about it. Family matters, you know," with trembling hand, she lifted her cup and took a sip.

"Bethany may have seen Bobby Riddling drown Roselyn Redmond," Jix blurted out.

Lucy's eyes widened. Easing her cup onto its saucer, she asked, "How can you say such a thing? How…how do you know?"

Jix, embarrassed she'd not been more tactful, chose her words carefully. She told Lucy what was recorded in the diary but did not say Bethany was very much alive and, in fact, nearby.

Abby Gayle said, "You know Bobby Riddling. Please tell us about him."

Like a gypsy reading tealeaves, Lucy gazed into the cup of brew she gripped with both hands. After a momentary deliberation, she replied, "We are a very private family. There are things we just don't talk about. Sorry, but I can't tell you Bobby or Laura's personal business. Suffice it to say, Laura's husband is a perplexing person."

Abby Gayle explained, "We don't want to pry into your family's private affairs. We are trying to understand who Bobby Riddling is. Is he the type of person who could drown an innocent girl?"

"That's right, Lucy. It is not our intention to meddle or intrude. But like it or not, there is an investigation in progress as to whether this man has committed a crime. The truth is going to come out," Jix said.

Lucy went to the sink to rinse her plate. "I would like to think he is incapable of such a horrible deed as you've suggested," she said over her shoulder before rejoining her uninvited guests.

Neither Jix nor Abby Gayle questioned further. The women sat in silence until Lucy was ready to talk about Bobby or tell them to leave.

The cat returned. Loud, intense meows shattered the silence, indicating delaying breakfast would no longer be tolerated. Lucy opened the door and let the yellow, furry fellow, whom she called Luther, inside.

While opening a can of cat food, she commented, "I don't live inside Bobby Riddling's head, so I don't know what he is capable of. My sister became involved with him when she was very young. She has always been faithful to her husband; however, on more than one occasion that I am aware of, he has not remained loyal to her."

She set a plate on the floor for the cat and then slid back into her chair across from her visitors seated at the banquette.

"Does Laura ever see him? Does he stay in touch with Paula or her sister?" Jix asked.

"Yes, Laura sees him when he chooses to grace her with his presence." Her gentle manner was not enough to disguise an angry tone. "Bobby phones Paula on holidays. Laura's youngest daughter, Peggy, lives in Jackson and sees her father once or twice a year. He is not a traditional family man."

Lucy hesitated as if trying to decide whether to share a matter weighing heavy on her heart. "As a matter of fact, Laura called early this morning to tell me Bobby is arriving in a few days...on Friday." She added sarcastically, "That he let her know is a novelty; he usually shows up unannounced."

"And Laura is all right with this arrangement?" Jix asked.

"She has no choice." Lucy changed the subject by offering coffee or tea refills; Jix handed over her cup.

With a sigh, Lucy tilted the coffee carafe. "My sister is a very fragile person. Rather than face reality, Laura chooses to see things...differently. She thinks if she doesn't acknowledge something, it simply ceases to exist. By living in the past, she avoids facing the present."

Lucy glanced at her watch. "Please excuse my rudeness, but I have an appointment, and I need to get dressed."

"We understand. But quickly, may I ask about your sister, Amelia? Detective Bird tells me anaphylactic shock due to bee venom has been established as the cause of death. Do you know if the bees belonged to her neighbor? Why would she have put herself in harm's way?" Jix said.

"A garden in a rural area surrounds a gazebo located between Amelia's property and her neighbor. She died near the gazebo. The apiary is located underneath trees in a meadow not far from both the house and the gazebo. It's a mystery as to why Amelia had gone there very early in the morning. Her husband was still in bed. She seldom went to the garden because it was a lengthy walk, and Amelia had back problems—old injury from a fall." Lucy looked away. "Sorry, I must see you out."

Amid good-byes at the back door, Jix held up her index finger. "You've been so kind and helpful. If you don't mind, may I ask one more thing, Lucy? If it can be proven Bobby Riddling had a hand in the deaths of Roselyn or Amelia, do you want to see your brother-in-law held accountable?'

"I can think of nothing I'd like better."

Chapter Twenty-Two

The Trunk Doctor's new helper proved to be a wise choice. Que was strong, he caught on quickly, and he was a fast worker. He could clean the metal on two trunks in the time it took Earl to clean one. Jix had hoped to hear Que's version of the boating accident in detail, but he seemed reluctant to discuss the incident, so she didn't press the matter.

Richard Manikin had called to ask if he might meet with Jix. He had suggested lunch, but instead, she'd invited him to drop by her house around four o'clock. Que's police escort picked him up at three, giving her plenty of time to clean up and take a break before Richard arrived.

He was on time and anxious to verify what Lucy had told him. Jix led her guest to a laundry room with a flickering fluorescent bulb she'd converted into a neat, well-organized office. She turned on the coffee maker and took a seat behind the desk. Richard sat in a chair facing her.

"Thanks for coming. I hope you don't mind meeting here." She'd wondered if Lucy would tell anyone of the accusations against her sister's husband.

"No. Not at all." He leaned back in the chair and looked around the room. "This appears to be quite adequate...and cozy. My first office was not much larger."

"I like it, and it's private," she added. "Before you leave, remind me to show you Betty Sue's trunk. The exterior is finished. The wood cleaned up nicely, and leather straps dress it up."

"I'm anxious to see it. My reason for wanting to get together is to clear up a bit of confusion. I want to ask you about your conversation with Aunt Lucy." He shifted to a more comfortable position before continuing. "What did you say to her concerning my father-in-law? I hope she has misunderstood."

"Sure. Glad you came by. I told Lucy that Bethany Perkins had written in her diary she'd seen Bobby Riddling drown Roselyn Redmond." Again, Jix hadn't intended to be so blunt. Quickly, her inner voice, in no uncertain terms, scolded her for her lack of sensitivity.

Richard was momentarily at a loss for words. He folded his hands in his lap, cleared his throat, and met Jix's gaze. "I'm certain you are aware this is a serious criminal accusation. Is there any evidence other than something written in a diary three decades ago? If not, perhaps you needn't press this issue any further."

Jix knew she was on thin ice. Revealing that Bethany was nearby could compromise the Quayling's safety. "Richard, I'm sorry, but I can't share any details. I will say there is also an eyewitness."

Richard bolted forward, "Eyewitness! Surely, you're joking! Who is this eyewitness?" Visibly shaken, he gripped the chair arms.

"I'm not at liberty to share information. May I ask you a question? Do you think your father-in-law is capable of deliberately drowning a young girl? You know him; I don't. Help me understand who he is. Talk to me about him."

Richard threw his hands in the air. "This is ridiculous! There is no jury in the land that would convict a person of murder based on what a teenager wrote in a diary thirty years ago. And even if there is a witness, a good lawyer...and let me assure you, my father-in-law can afford the best...would discredit a witness in a heartbeat."

"I agree. To be honest with you, I don't know where this is headed. At this point the evidence is flimsy, to say the least. There are more questions than answers." An uneasy niggling as to where Richard's loyalties lie cautioned Jix to refrain from confiding in him. "I could better understand if I knew the person accused. Tell me about Bobby Riddling."

Unsure of what she wanted to hear, Richard began, "There's not much to tell. He's different. He's distant. He wants to have his cake and eat it too. He's a power player. He was never a loving, devoted father to Paula and Peggy and certainly not a traditional husband to Mom Riddling. Oh, he isn't physically abusive to her, and in his own way, he may love her. On occasion, he has been impatient with her, yet he is more tolerant of her than he is Paula or Aunt Lucy. However—with all due respect—Mom Riddling could try the patience of a saint." He paused. "I don't know of anyone he is close to. On the other hand, he can be hospitable...even charming. He is a genius when it comes to making money." As an afterthought, he added, "And he doesn't hide that he has a roving eye. He comes and goes as he pleases. She thinks he is away on business trips."

"If he has committed this crime, do you want to see him held accountable?"

"Of course! Without a doubt! Albeit, Robert Riddling's welfare is not my greatest concern. Paula is my greatest concern. I don't want her to suffer through an accusation that cannot be proven. All that would do is cause unnecessary heartache for her...and our girls. Where is Avonelle on all this?"

"She is investigating. And I may as well tell you; a question has arisen as to whether Mr. Riddling may also have been involved in Amelia's death. So far, this is speculation on the behalf of one person." She was satisfied to have at least rendered an effort to deliver this newsflash in a more civil manner.

Even so, Richard's drop-jaw expression of disbelief triggered an urge to give the man a moment.

Jix sprang to her feet, "I made coffee. Let's take a break and have a cup." Before her guest could comment, she walked around the desk to the coffee station. "Cream and sugar?" she asked.

"No. Nothing. Black."

She filled two mugs while Richard mulled over their conversation. "Lucy tells me Laura's husband will be here on Friday," Jix said.

"That's what I hear. He shows up from time to time, usually when he wants something."

"Does he stay overnight?" A stream of milk turned the dark brew light. She added sugar cubes to her cup and handed her guest the undoctored one.

Richard reached for the mug and took a sip. "Your guess is as good as mine. He usually doesn't let Mom Riddling know when he's coming. This is his first visit since she moved here. He has always owned a lake house and an apartment near his office, so she is accustomed to him being away for days, sometimes weeks. He may be planning to stay two or three hours or two or three days. I only know he called to say he will be here on Friday. I assume being as he is to arrive in late afternoon, he will stay overnight, but that's merely an assumption." He sat the cup on the desk.

"I'm somewhat puzzled at their marriage arrangement."

"Mom Riddling moved here at Aunt Lucy and Paula's insistence. Aunt Lucy knows better than anyone how to help her. I manage her personal affairs, and I have power of attorney to act on her behalf. My father-in-law provides a generous monthly allowance for Mom. If she needs more, I contact the Riddling's accountant, and he deposits into her account."

Jix contemplated the man sitting across from her. She had no choice but to go on her gut feeling. Based on instinct and basic rationale, she decided to trust him.

"If Detective Bird knows he is in town, she'll want to question him. Everything will be out in the open," she said.

Richard shook his head. "I'm telling you, Jix; all a police interview would accomplish is to put him on the offensive, and that's when he will turn suspicions into a joke. Based on what you have told me, you've got nothing. Not a shred of evidence to convict him of a crime. Short of a confession, you'll never pin anything on him. This is a waste of time, and I don't want Paula hurt."

The phone rang. Jix answered and told her mother she would be in as soon as she finished. A brief chat about supper ended with Margee saying she would get things started. When Jix hung up, Richard said he needed to be on his way.

Jix knew Bill would be angry if she didn't mind her own business and let the police handle the investigation. She also knew he'd get over it eventually. While an alleged murderer was within reach, she had to do what she could to trap him.

"If you'd really like to bring this to a head before Paula returns, perhaps together, we could come up with a plan." She had his attention. "Are you in?"

"I'm in," he said, without hesitation. "What do you have in mind?"

"First and foremost, we must get Detective Bird's authorization and cooperation. We'll need to meet with her tomorrow." Jix wanted to abide by the letter of the law.

"She's flexible," Richard said. "She'll listen."

Chapter Twenty-Three

Rubber tires griped gravel; gears growled like a watchdog. Aiming to avoid sliding onto narrow or non-existing shoulders, a white-knuckled driver steadily climbed along the steep, washed-out road. Destination: the log house on the ridge.

Jix kept her eyes on the road while she spoke. "Que is working on the big steamer trunk. You know the one I picked up at the truck stop on the Interstate when I met those people who were on their way to Florida? It's a rush job. They're staying at the beach for two weeks and will get the trunk on their way back home."

"Where do they live?"

"Connecticut."

Abby Gayle remembered the tall, stand-alone trunk with drawers stacked on one side and space to hang clothes on the other.

"We'll have Bethany to ourselves. There are a few things I want to discuss in her husband's absence," Jix said.

It was unlikely another car would approach from the opposite direction; even so, she was prepared to swerve from the center of the road back into the right-hand lane.

"Does she know we're coming?"

"No. I didn't tell anyone. I asked Bill how to get to the house. I didn't ask like I needed directions because I was going to go to the house but as a matter of general interest."

"Seriously? You know he knew you were coming up here."

"He probably knew. He didn't want to hear me say I was going to."

Following Bill's directions, the girls finally located the obscured driveway snaking through the woods to the house. They parked in front and knocked on the door. Sopakco answered.

"The lady of the house isn't in," he informed the visitors from behind the door he'd barely cracked open.

The familiar reply used by English butlers in classic Hollywood movies fell on deaf ears.

"Oh, but she is. Officer Sopakco, I'm Jix Haynes, and this is Abby Gayle Kamp. I'm working very closely with Detective Bird on this case," Jix said.

Unable to keep from rolling her eyes, Abby Gayle turned her back on the man peeping out the door.

Jix continued. "We're close friends of Bethany and her husband. My husband owns this house, and I have permission to be here. May we come in?"

"Let me give Detective Bird a call." Sopakco started to close the door to phone.

In the wink of an eye, Jix gently butted her shoulder against the door, stepped inside, and shouted, "Bethany!

Hello, Bethany! It's Jix and Abby Gayle. We've come to see if you need anything!"

Bethany appeared and assured her bodyguard the women harbored no ill intent. Sopakco glared at Jix. She offered an apologetic smile and followed their hostess into the kitchen.

The guests commented on the house while Bethany offered refreshments and loaded the coffee maker. "Do you have everything you need? Although one might say it is a wee bit off the beaten path, the house is very nice," said Jix.

"It is Buckingham Palace to us. Serve yourselves cake, or I have cookies if you prefer. I'll bring the coffee, and we'll move to the screened porch." Bethany led the way, closing the sliding doors before Sopakco could join them. "Please don't think I'm ungrateful," she said to the ladies, "but our protector is like a second skin. He is ever-present. I know this is necessary, but we have no privacy."

Abby Gayle set her plate on a table beside a sofa stuffed with cushions covered in striped canvas before surveying the amazing view. "Surely it won't be much longer before Detective Bird completes her investigation," she said.

Bethany backed up to the swing and sat down. Her eyes swept the majestic mountains on the far side of the canyon. "I've told her what I saw; what is there to investigate?"

Jix detected the absence of the relieved, hopeful Bethany she had recently come to know. This Bethany was sad, tired, and moody.

"The cake is delicious," Jix took a bite before answering.

"Sopakco got it at the grocery store. I don't have what I'd need to bake a cake. I have ample time to bake enough cakes to supply a bakery." She folded her arms and gently rocked the swing with her foot.

Boredom and isolation were wearing on Bethany. Jix offered a solution. "To break the monotony, would you like to cut patterns from wallpaper? I use them to decorate trunks. I can send things with Que to give you something to do during the day. I mean, if it would help pass the time and it would help me. It's entirely up to you."

"Sure," she expressed lukewarm interest. "Tell him what you want me to do, and I'll do the best I can."

Jix followed up on Bethany's question, "As for the investigation, we need something more than your account of what happened to Roselyn. No one doubts your word, but it will all boil down to your word against his...unless he confesses."

Abby Gayle set down a half-full mug and leaned forward. "Bethany, the police are looking into the circumstances of Amelia's death. What exactly makes you think Bobby Riddling had anything to do with it? Did he and Amelia keep in touch over the years? We've heard more than once these people are not a close family."

The swing bumped the wall when, without warning, Bethany sprang to her feet. She jabbed her hands deep into her pants' pocket and paced the length of the porch. A glance at Sopakco on the other side of the glass doors prompted a wave that all was well. He backed away and leaned against the kitchen counter while keeping a close eye on the ladies.

"Please sit down. We didn't come to upset you," Jix put her arm around the distraught woman's shoulder and led her to the swing. Both sat down.

Bethany blinked back tears. "Will this ever truly end? I want to be able to go about my business without looking over my shoulder. I want to sleep at night without someone on the other side of the bedroom door watching for intruders. I want a home. I want a normal life! I've lived half my life or more, and I have nothing to show for it." Tears streamed down her cheeks.

Sopakco opened the door. "What's going on? You want these two to leave?"

Bethany pulled a tissue from her pocket and dried her eyes. "It's okay. It's okay. I'm a little on edge, but I'll be okay." At her insistence, he stepped back inside. She begged their pardon to ample reassurance from the ladies they understood.

"It will be over soon," Jix told her. "But we have to be certain Mr. Riddling doesn't wiggle out of this. Eventually, Detective Bird will question him and present the diary as evidence, but that alone isn't going to stand up in court. A jury will never convict him. We have to work together and set a trap."

Bethany snapped to attention, "A trap?" Wide-eyed, she questioned.

Abby Gayle added, "You have to tell us everything. Everything. There are a couple of questions we need answered. Are you up to discussing these things now?"

"Yes," she stated. "I'll answer as honestly as possible."

As honestly as possible? For the moment, Jix didn't explore Bethany's phrasing any further, but she wondered why a person with so much on the line would hesitate to answer sincerely. What would prohibit her telling the truth?

Chapter Twenty-Four

"Bethany, why did you take the shoes and the lock of hair that were inside the trunk? Why those things and nothing else?" Abby Gayle had waited for the right moment to confront the person who had broken into the box stored in her garage.

"The shoes belonged to my mother and, before her, my grandmother."

Bethany stood and looked through the wire screen enclosing the porch. The beauty of the vast, cavernous pit fenced by tree-covered mountains was mesmerizing.

"I miss her. She gave the shoes to me when I was sixteen and told me to keep them in the family. She thought someday I would have a little girl who would treasure them."

Jix asked, "Is your mother still living?"

Bethany answered, "Yes, but to protect her, I haven't contacted her in years." She added as an afterthought, "My dad passed away when I was a freshman in high school. His death was devastating to our family."

She turned to face her visitors.

"And the lock of hair is from a little girl I loved." She frowned and once again looked across to the far mountain range.

When no further comments were forthcoming, Abby Gayle asked, "Whose child?"

She hesitated before replying, "Amelia's."

"Start at the beginning and tell us about Amelia. Tell us the truth, Bethany. Not the truth as much as possible but tell us the whole truth. It will all come out as this unfolds."

Bethany inhaled deeply and sat down on the swing. She leaned back and looked away from the women as she talked. "It was all so long ago," she said, to herself more than to those listening.

"Laura and Bobby had not been married long before he became inappropriately friendly with Amelia. She and I were kids. Laura and Amelia's father had died, and their mother was seriously ill. I told Laura what Bobby was doing, but she would not believe me. She instead accused me of everything she could think of...taking her things or doing things I didn't do. I think she argued with me so I wouldn't tell her bad things about her husband. She was so different from Lucy or anyone that I knew. Her family excused her erratic behavior and acted as if she just had a quirky personality."

Jix asked, "Why didn't you tell someone else? Your mother or Lucy?"

"Laura threatened me if I told anyone what Bobby was doing. I was so young, she was so convincing, and I was afraid of her. Frankly, I think everyone who knew her was a little afraid of what she might do. Laura had an evil look that terrified me. She would grab my shoulders and shake me so hard it hurt. I didn't know what to do. When Amelia became pregnant, Laura swore us both to secrecy. Amelia was afraid of her too."

Caught by surprise, Jix asked, "What happened to the baby?"

"Laura kept the baby and raised the little girl as her own. Amelia went away several months before the baby was born so no one would know; everyone thought she was away at school. Laura and Bobby moved away for a year or so. Supposedly, he was taking business courses at the university."

Jix was astounded. "Paula?" she ventured a guess.

Bethany explained. "Yes, that is why Amelia left the trunk to Paula. She wanted her daughter to have it. Even though it is my trunk, Amelia didn't know how to find me. Bobby and Laura moved away and cut ties with Amelia. They may have visited once or twice over the years, but the Riddlings kept Paula away from her biological mother. Amelia married and had other children, but she always grieved for her baby who had been taken from her. She loved Paula, as I did…and still do."

Abby Gayle asked, "And Roselyn—Bobby Riddling impregnated her too?"

"Yes. I tried to warn Roselyn. I couldn't tell her about Amelia's baby, but I begged her to tell her mother she was going to have a baby. She said she would, but she wanted to tell Bobby first; she told him at the picnic." She paused reflectively. "He drowned her. I saw him hold her under the water." Bethany began to sob. Jix gathered her in her arms, and they both wept.

When tears were wiped away, Jix issued an invitation. "I'm having an important meeting at my house tonight, and I'm asking you and Sopakco to go back to town with us now. Que will stay after he finishes work. Others are meeting with us, Detective Bird included. With a little luck and a lot of strategizing, we are about to give Mr. Riddling a dose of his own medicine. Bethany, I need you to be braver than you've ever been. We have one shot at putting this bozo away once and for all."

When Jix considered the woman she was speaking to had been an impersonator, a thief, and a hit-and-run driver, she was confident Bethany would be able, with a little help, to catch a killer.

Chapter Twenty-Five

"So, let me get this straight. While I was on my way home from a meeting in Atlanta, you were in our den organizing a sting operation?" He turned off the light on his side of the bed and wiggled into a comfortable position. Every muscle in Bill Haynes' tired body began to release tension like a slow leak in a punctured tire.

"More or less." From her side of the bed, Jix mindlessly focused on the ceiling fan silhouetted in a yellow glow from moonlight streaming through the window. "I wouldn't go so far as to call this a sting operation, not technically. I'm told it is important to avoid entrapment."

"Oh, I see. Would it not be better to leave this sort of thing entirely up to people who are trained to catch criminals? Just a suggestion."

"Sure, it would, but there's no time. Bobby Riddling is coming to town tomorrow. If our plan works, we may be able to nail him for both Roselyn and Amelia's deaths. It's a long shot, but we have to try." Jix was too excited to sleep. It wasn't every day she exposed an unsolved murder and came face-to-face with the alleged killer.

She continued, "Besides, Avonelle has agreed to help. Well, not just help. She is in charge…more or less." She turned on her side to face her husband. "And there is a possibility Amelia may have been blackmailing Riddling. Somehow, Richard found out a chunk of change was deposited in Amelia's account for three months before her death. They are looking for matching withdrawals from Bobby's bank. Apparently, Mr. Riddling has multiple business interests and, therefore, multiple bank accounts."

"Avonelle. Now it's Avonelle, not Detective Bird. Jix, you are overstepping boundaries. I can't believe you are involved in this mess."

"Believe it." She scrunched the pillow and sunk into its downy softness.

Bill wanted to avoid additional stimulating conversation so he could get to sleep; even so, he had to ask, "Last I heard, you weren't certain Riddling was coming. Lucy told you the man is very unpredictable. Have you considered he may not even show up?"

"Richard said it is a sure thing; he will definitely be at Laura's. Richard, Bobby, and Laura are going out to dinner. And Lucy. I assume her husband too, but I don't know for sure. You do remember tomorrow is Mother's birthday, and we have reservations for dinner?"

Bill turned toward his wife. "Oh, Lord have mercy! Please don't tell me they're eating at Ramone's. And I'd be willing to bet they'll be there when we are."

"They are, and they will, but I won't tell you. Sweet dreams, darling. Don't worry. I'll fill you in on a few important details in the morning. Let's get to sleep." She tenderly kissed him goodnight.

142

0—¬

Richard arrived early at the car dealership and slipped in the back way hoping no one would see him. He'd left the house before Lucy arrived for the day, and he'd gone through a fast food drive-thru to get coffee and breakfast. Upcoming events demanded he find uninterrupted time to think.

All this business with his father-in-law had him on edge. Truth be known, he was always jittery when in the presence of Paula's father, even though he could not say any single event had triggered this sense of trepidation. It stemmed from years of observing his in-laws' unusual-in-a-strange-way habits.

Richard knew *about* Robert Riddling, but he didn't *know* the man. To add to the mix, his mother-in-law had an inability to cope with life's ordinary demands. None of this was his prime concern. Protecting Paula and their children was all Richard really cared about.

He pried the lid off the paper cup and blew on the hot coffee before taking a sip. Leaning back in his swivel chair, he listened to the phone ring while he waited for Lucy to answer.

"Hello."

"Morning, Aunt Lucy. Hope I'm not calling too early."

"Of course not, dear. We're finishing breakfast, and then I'm off to your house. I'll stop on the way to pick up a few things I need from the store. And I'll check in on Laura. She has a hair appointment this morning." She loaded the dishwasher with one hand while holding the phone to her ear with the other.

"Have you talked to Mom Riddling? Are we still on for dinner tonight?"

Lucy filled her cup and pushed the off button on the coffeemaker. "I talked with her last night. She thinks Bobby is returning from a business trip to England. She's excited, and she's looking forward to dining at Ramone's."

"Do we know for certain he still plans to come today?"

"Far as I know. From what I gather, he will play in the golf tournament on Saturday and Sunday. I suspect the tournament is more than likely the reason for his visit. As you know, this is his first visit since she moved here."

"He could stay in a hotel if the tournament is the only reason he is in town. She would never know he is in the area."

"Of course, he could, but I think making an appearance eases his conscience. I've often wondered if he strayed from Laura because he couldn't bear to see her becoming more fragile emotionally and mentally. Or did his roving eye cause her to flee further from reality?"

Richard turned his chair to face the bookcase. The photographic mosaic of his wife and their beautiful daughters reminded him where his heart was anchored.

"I don't know, Aunt Lucy. I do know I don't want Paula to have to suffer through a lengthy investigation, which may do nothing more than stir up a stink. If her father has committed murder, I want to see it proven and him held accountable as quickly as possible."

"I agree whole-heartedly. We'll meet at Laura's at seven; our dinner reservations are for seven-thirty. Jix has a surprise, and no matter what happens, we are to play along."

Chapter Twenty-Six

Door chimes declared Mr. Riddling's arrival. Laura, brimming with delight, rushed to welcome him with open arms.

The broad-shouldered, tall man with thick, sterling strands of hair kissed her forehead.

"Come in, my darling. How was your trip? I want to hear all about it. Don't leave out a single detail." She waited for him to gather his valise then led the way inside.

He glanced about the foyer before speaking. "You look nice, Laura."

"Oh, thank you." She twirled around to show off her dress. "Welcome home. I've missed you."

He left his satchel in the foyer and entered the parlor. Looking about, he said, "This is so…you."

"I knew you'd love it," she replied.

He chuckled.

"Dear, dear, Laura. Come and tell me what you've been doing." They had no sooner sat down side-by-side on the sofa until the black cats appeared from behind the door.

"No cats, Laura. If they stay, I'll go. You know I can't tolerate animals inside the house. I reminded you when I called," he sternly rebuked her.

She jumped to her feet, "Oh, no! I locked them in the bedroom. I don't know how they've gotten out. I'm so sorry, Bobby, so sorry." Bumping into the coffee table, she clapped her hands to drive the felines into the kitchen. Once she'd deposited them down the basement stairs, she returned.

"I'm so sorry." She repeated, nervously smoothing her hair. "I can't imagine how they got out. I'm sure I closed the door." Anxious to change the subject, she glanced at her watch. "We have time to visit before you dress for dinner. Lucy may stop by beforehand, and Richard will come for us at seven."

He patted the sofa for her to sit beside him and then told her what she wanted to hear. A trip to England unfolded with details of a day spent at Covent Gardens, even though it had been two years since he'd been in London. He described the street entertainers and the craft shops at the Apple Market and the Royal Opera House. Laura hung on to every word, laughing and commenting.

A finger went to his lips and she quieted. Making a fist, he slowly stretched his hand forward and reached behind her head.

"Abracadabra," he whispered. With considerable virtuosity, he withdrew his hand and slowly unfurled his fingers to reveal a small box perched on his palm.

Charmed and fascinated, Laura clapped with glee. Her nimble fingers tore the wrappings and put the lid aside. An exquisite ruby and diamond bracelet rested on a bed of white satin.

"Bobby, I love it!" she exclaimed, as he fastened the dazzling circle on her wrist. "And I love you." She threw her arms around his neck.

"I hope you enjoy wearing it," he said. Happiness had been the reaction he'd expected.

With one finger, she played with the bracelet, sliding it around her tiny wrist. Dropping her hands in her lap, she leaned forward to say endearingly, "I tried to do something for you, but I don't think I was successful."

"What are you talking about? What have you done?"

She tossed her head and lifted her chin. A mischievous smile spread her lips. "I had visitors."

Holding her arm in mid air, she admired the bracelet. When she continued to play with it, he asked, "What visitors, Laura?'

Before she could answer, the doorbell rang. Laura jumped to her feet and rushed to greet Lucy.

"Come and see who's here, dear sister."

Certain telltale signs in her sister's behavior caught Lucy's attention. She considered excitement over Bobby's return as the cause, but to be safe, she asked if Laura had taken her medication at noon. She hadn't, so Lucy brought a pill and a glass of water and watched while Laura took it. She chatted briefly with Bobby and then bade the two farewell until the dinner hour.

"Come, sit down." Bobby patted the sofa cushion as Laura rejoined him.

He stroked her hand and then touched her knuckles with his lips. "Who visited, sweetheart? You said you had visitors, and you tried to do something for me."

She thought for a moment, "Visitors?"

"Take your time. It will come to you. Who has visited lately?"

Suddenly, she reconnected with her previous train of thought. "Oh, yes. Two ladies came for tea. They had a diary that had belonged to Bethany. They found it in Amelia's old trunk." Her eyes glistened. "I knew they were up to no good. I attempted to poison them with Edgar Allan and Poe's catnip scones, so they can't hurt you, but I don't think I was successful. I'm sorry, dear one; I tried."

She wrung her trembling hands. "Don't tell Lucy what I've done. She will be very upset."

Chapter Twenty-Seven

Spirited, ebullient chatter from Friday night diners muffled background mood music. Every table was occupied or reserved, leaving those without a reservation to wait in the cramped foyer of Ramone's Restaurant. Waiters with black bow ties and white shirts darted about balancing food-laden trays as effortlessly as a woman carries her purse.

Weaving through the noisy, crowded room, Abby Gayle and Austin spotted Bill, Jix, Margee, and Carol seated in a corner booth at a table set for six.

"Happy birthday, Margee!" The Kamps contributed to a rise in the sound level as they greeted dear friends. Jix scooted over, making room for Abby Gayle. Austin shook hands with Bill and kissed Margee's cheek before he sat down.

The birthday girl had enjoyed a day of gifts, cake, and best wishes from friends and family near and far. Her plans to finish off a perfect celebration included lobster and steak and, if there was room, a tiramisu.

Abby Gayle leaned close to Jix. "Are they here yet?"

She gestured toward the reserved table across from them. "That's their table." She slid her cuff up to look at her watch. "They should be here soon."

"And Detective Bird?"

Jix raised a brow and spoke nonverbally with her eyes.

A surprised Abby Gayle followed Jix's gaze that had landed across the room on Avonelle Bird with menus in hand, seating a couple. "Where's Irene? I saw her when we came in," she inquired as to the whereabouts of the regular hostess whom she knew well.

"She's over there. Detective Bird is working undercover."

Abby Gayle giggled. "Oh, really. And I suppose that's why Detective Martino is dressed as a waiter." She referred to the man bussing a table nearby.

Their waiter was Justin, a young man who'd obviously graduated head of his class in Customer-Pleasing 101. "How is everybody tonight?" he gaily inquired as if he actually cared.

Upon learning of a birthday celebration, Justin conveyed well wishes and news of a free dessert. He'd taken drink orders and was about to leave when Detective Bird escorted a party of five to the reserved table.

Richard caught Bill's eye, waved hello, and led the members of his party to a round of introductions. Lucy's husband Lester greeted everyone and then sat down at the reserved table to look over the menu while the others socialized. Laura joined him as soon as she'd spoken to everyone. Surprised to find the catnip scone survivors were Richard's friends, she was nervous and anxious to tell Bobby.

150

When introduced to Bobby Riddling, Jix said hello to the man who responded with a polite greeting.

She had mentally rehearsed a face-to-face encounter a dozen times or more. Never once did she think she would be caught off guard, but as their eyes met, Jix discovered she was not as prepared as she had imagined.

Accused murderer Bobby Riddling had evolved from a mental image to become as real as life, and close enough to poke with a finger.

He didn't look dangerous. Au contraire, he was a well-groomed man; one might even say handsome. Had she met him under other circumstances she might have thought him to be a senator, a bank president, or dean of a university. His engaging manner and charm contradicted every unsavory trait she'd expected to find.

Lucy lingered to chat with Carol and Margee about an upcoming community theatre production. Richard and Bobby rejoined Laura and Lester to find they'd both decided on seared filet mignon with Pinot sauce, cassoulet of chanterelle, and lobster.

Justin arrived with drinks and a loaf of freshly baked oat/wheat bread wafing a nostril tingling, yeasty aroma. Bill sliced the warm bread and passed it around the table. Carol and Margee continued to talk about the play auditions after Lucy had rejoined her family. Golfers Bill and Austin discussed Saturday's golf tournament.

Abby Gayle buttered a slice of bread. "Jix, want bread? It's hot and delicious."

"No thanks," she sipped iced tea.

"What's the matter?"

"Nothing. I'm trying to reconcile the gap between the Bobby Riddling we've heard so much about and the man I just met. How close have I come to the truth of who he is?" She absentmindedly broke off a piece of bread even though she'd said she didn't want any.

Abby Gayle passed the butter. "Truly. It's surreal."

"What if he didn't do anything to Roselyn or Amelia? What if Bethany didn't see a drowning? He could have been trying to save her rather than drown her. And what if Amelia's death was clearly a case of being in the wrong place at the wrong time?"

"Seriously? Where is all this second-guessing coming from?" Abby Gayle laid the butter knife across the bread plate and turned to look Jix squarely in the eye.

"He doesn't look like a killer." Jix spoke barely above a whisper as the others in the semi-circular booth conversed with the person sitting next to them.

With one brow lifted, Abby Gayle heaved a sigh. "And what does a killer look like? Do they all have a "killer-look" in their eyes? Are there standard characteristics that warn who is a murderer? Ted Bundy didn't look like a killer, but he was. Not every killer is a street thug or a lunatic."

Jix could not argue with her reasoning. Abby Gayle had once again rescued her from a tendency to over think. She changed the subject; "It'll be interesting to see his reaction when Bethany arrives."

Chapter Twenty-Eight

And she did indeed arrive—Bethany, that is. But not until everyone had enjoyed a delicious, satisfying meal. Richard issued an invitation to stop by his house after dinner for a drink. Carol opted out, saying she had to relieve the babysitter. Margee also declined the invitation stating if she intended to live to see another birthday, she would need to rest from this one. Knowing Lucy would stay half the night, Lester had driven his car while Lucy drove hers. He wanted to see *Miami Vice* at ten.

Austin he needed to get to bed early in order to get on the road at the crack of dawn. Bill took a rain check on Richard's offer simply because he was ready to go home; Jix could ride with Abby Gayle.

At first, the Riddlings begged off, saying Bobby needed to get to bed early in order to play in Saturday's golf tournament. Richard insisted it was still early with plenty

153

of time for one drink. Reluctantly, they agreed, stipulating they could only stay a short time.

As Lucy gathered her purse and a take-out box of leftover shrimp, hostess-for-a-night Avonelle Bird approached with a couple in tow. She led the two to Richard's table then stepped aside, lingering nearby.

"Hey, what do you know; it's the Hallmarks! How delightful!" Richard stood to shake hands with Bobby Quayling, as if they were dear friends.

Adrenaline flushed Richard's system as he played his part in a risky charade. "Steve. Barbara. How nice to run into you. Let me introduce you to everyone."

Lester dismissed the couple with little more than a glance then forked an overlooked bite of steak.

Lucy, Laura, and Bobby locked eyes with the woman. Time had erased recognition and replaced it with an uneasy sense of familiarity. When none of the three spoke, she did. "It's a pleasure to make your acquaintance," Bethany said politely.

Que followed suit. "Same here," he said.

Laura squeezed her husband's leg underneath the table.

Lucy was startled but quickly regained composure. "Lovely to meet you both," she said. Somewhat embarrassed at her initial response, she offered an explanation. "Barbara, you bear a striking resemblance to an acquaintance we haven't seen in more than thirty years." She turned to her brother-in-law, "Doesn't she, Bobby?"

He lowered his gaze then looked up to speak. "Yes. Yes, she does." He furrowed his brow. With clinched jaw, he said, "And you Steve...you look familiar. Ever been in the Jackson, Mississippi area?"

Even though she was a seasoned impersonator, Bethany was unnerved. She was, after all, facing her demon of mental anguish. So far, the woman's performance would assure her an Oscar.

Before Que could answer, Jix and Bill suddenly appeared on the scene, followed by Abby Gayle and Austin. "Barbara Hallmark! How nice to see you!" Jix, supporting actress in the ongoing deceptive plot, offered a comfort-hug as a greeting.

Austin shook hands with Que, "Hey, Steve. How's it going?"

"Doing good. We've eaten a fantastic dinner, and we're on our way home," he said.

Richard seized the opportunity, "You folks are just in time. We're stopping off at my house for drinks. You guys join us. I insist! I won't take no for an answer. Steve, you're playing in tomorrow's tournament, aren't you? You and my father-in-law will have lots to talk about."

Que wasn't a golfer nor did he know much about the game; he grinned in lieu of a comment.

Jix and Abby Gayle also insisted Barbara and Steve join them. Finally, it was settled; everyone would stop by Richard's for a nightcap.

"It'll be fun. Follow me," Richard said to his in-laws, Abby Gayle, Jix, and the Quaylings.

Chapter Twenty-Nine

Bad weather seemed a sure thing, judging from thunder rumbling in the distance and frequent flashes of lightning ripping across a starless sky.

"Looks like a storm's brewing." Abby Gayle followed close behind Richard's car; the headlights projected silhouettes of Richard and Bobby in front and the twin sisters in the backseat.

Jix peered up at the dark, troubled sky. "In more ways than one. However, the restaurant reveal went off without a hitch. It was a good idea to reunite the Riddlings with Bethany in a public place. It will give them wiggle room to plan their next move."

Jix thought out loud, "I wanted to warn Lucy, but I also wanted to see her reaction when she saw Bethany. I'm convinced she has told us all she knows about the graduation picnic and the events that took place. It has

157

been a challenge determining which of these people can be trusted."

Lights from Sopakco's vehicle danced in the rearview mirror. Once he had dropped off Bethany and Que at Richard's front door, he would circle round and come in the back way. Detectives Bird and Martino were already hiding inside, waiting for the entourage to arrive.

The girls speculated on the conversation taking place in Richard's car. "They may want to discuss the possibility Barbara could be Bethany, but they may hesitate to talk with Richard present," Abby Gayle turned on the windshield wipers to sweep away sprinkling rain.

Jix calculated audibly, "If they haven't seen her since she was eighteen, and she is fifty...let's see...it's nineteen eighty-nine, and the picnic was in nineteen fifty-seven...."

Abby Gayle laughed. "I know this isn't funny but wondering if Barbara is Bethany Perkins and if Steve is Bobby Quayling must be as unsettling as opening the closet door and finding rattling skeletons."

"We need to be prepared for anything."

Richard's brake lights flashed bright red. Abby Gayle slowed and flipped on the turn indicator.

Jix said, "With any luck, if we play along, he will hang himself. You engage Lucy in conversation, I'll keep Laura busy, and Richard is in charge of Que, who knows he is to follow Richard's lead. That leaves Mr. Riddling to catch up on old times with Barbara...Bethany."

The rain had quickly increased from a sprinkle to a steady downpour, requiring a mad dash to the front porch from cars parked in single file along a curved driveway. A curtain of raindrops veiled the lampposts and porch light at Laura's house across the street.

By the glow of the porch fixture, Richard unlocked the door and reached inside to flip the switch to the chandelier in the foyer. Everyone shook off as much water as possible on the doormat and while stomping rain soaked shoes, they hurried inside.

"Aunt Lucy, will you please get towels?" To the others shedding wet apparel he said, "We heard on the car radio there are severe thunderstorm warnings for the area. Did anybody know storms were predicted for today? I didn't."

"I haven't turned on the television today, but Bill did mention the possibility of bad weather. He didn't elaborate, and I didn't think anymore about it." Jix had had events scheduled for later in the day on her mind, and little else.

Lucy and Abby Gayle knew of thunderstorm warnings but thought they were expected after midnight.

Laura pulled on her husband's arm. "We need to go home, Bobby," she whined. "You know I'm terrified of storms."

Abby Gayle stood on tiptoes to look through the peephole at rain pounding on the porch. "It's pouring down, Mrs. Riddling. Perhaps you'd better wait a while until the rain lets up."

Bobby put his arm around Laura's shoulder. "There's nothing to be afraid of, Laura. It's a passing storm, and you know a storm will not harm you. Settle down. Before you know it, skies will be clear, and stars will twinkle."

Lucy hugged her sister and offered reassurance before stepping into the powder room to retrieve hand towels. Richard asked Que to help tend bar and led the way while the others dried off, then followed.

Laura clung to Bobby as the two sat down on the sofa. He and his wife slid over to make room when Bethany sat down on the opposite end.

Startling everyone, the lights flickered. "Please excuse me," Lucy spoke over rumbling thunder. "I'm going to check on Harmony and Halo. They're upstairs, and I know they are frightened by the storm."

Abby Gayle's quizzical expression elicited an explanation. "Welsh Corgis. They supposedly belong to the children, but I think Richard is more attached to them than anyone else in this family."

"Probably so," he admitted from across the room at his station behind the bar. "A wife, five daughters, and two female dogs...and I hear it's supposed to be a man's world."

Que laughed with Richard. He sat the drinks he'd mixed on the bar and selected glasses for himself and Bethany. A teetotaler, ginger ale over ice with a twist of lemon or a strawberry was his wife's preference.

"Barbara, what would you like to drink?" Richard asked, when he delivered drinks to Laura and Bobby.

"Ginger ale, if you have it, please."

"Coming right up. One ginger ale, Steve," he shouted to the bartender.

Que came around with the already filled glass and handed it to Bethany. Richard turned on the television to check for weather alerts. He and Que sat at the bar, swiveling the stools to a comfortable angle for easy viewing.

Abby Gayle asked if she might tag along with Lucy. The place was packed with exquisite antiques, and the grandeur of the big house had piqued her interest. She wanted to see more. At the top of the stairs, they heard whining and barking from dogs behind closed doors.

Local Meteorologist James Tracey popped up on the screen. The familiar weatherman was in his element. Dark-haired with a matching mustache, dressed in a sport coat, shirt, and tie, he spit out facts with the speed of an auctioneer about thick cloud cover and storms as he tracked activity on an animated map.

James reported, "The National Weather Service has issued a severe thunderstorm warning until 2 a. m. for Jackson County and surrounding areas. Local Doppler radar indicates this is a real rainmaker. Expect possible hail and power outages...."

"Oh, my! Oh, my! No! No!" Laura buried her face in her hands, fearfully agonizing over a catastrophic outcome to the worsening weather situation. Her glass tumbled to the floor when she jumped to her feet, spilling most of her drink in her lap. Both her husband and Jix hurried to comfort her. Bobby folded her in his arms and stroked her hair in a calming effort.

"Ssshhhhh. Hush, Laura. Hush," he repeated over and over.

Once she settled down, Jix touched her shoulder and said, "Mrs. Riddling. Would you like to go upstairs and find Lucy? The storm is quickly passing through. Let's stick together, and before you know it, the rain will have stopped." She held Laura's hand and waited for an answer. "I haven't seen all of Paula's house. Perhaps you can show me around," she cheerfully added.

Laura dried her eyes on a napkin Bethany had given her and then agreed in an ambivalent tone. "I'm so sorry," she said. "Please forgive me. I need to find Lucy. Where is she?" she asked.

Jix reassured Bobby she would take care of the frightened woman. He acknowledged with a nod and spoke softly to his wife, "Sounds like an excellent idea, Laura. Lucy is probably wondering if you are looking for her. This nice lady will help you find her."

Chapter Thirty

The storm continued to intensify, inside as well as outside the house. Sheets of rain lashed against the windowpanes like angry waves slapping the sides of a boat. Huddling in the upstairs reading nook, Lucy, Laura, Abby Gayle, and Jix listened to echoing thunder rumble overhead. The windows rattled when lightning struck nearby, sending the dogs scampering for cover. Harmony sprung into Jix's lap. Abby Gayle caught Halo in mid air as she scrambled to get into the chair with her.

Laura once again burst into tears and threw her arms around Lucy.

Although her sister sought to comfort her, the distraught little woman was inconsolable.

"Stop this, Sister! Stop right now!" she sharply commanded. Laura swallowed a sob and blinked away tears.

"Come with me. Let's go to Paula's room, and you can lie down. I'll sit with you. You'll be more comfortable. Come on, Laura," she coaxed.

Holding Laura's hand, Lucy led the way to the bedroom. Harmony jumped from Jix's lap. Halo, with no intention of being left behind, followed.

Fingers splayed, Jix held her palms upward to gesture that things appeared to be veering off course.

When Lucy had shut the bedroom door, Abby Gayle leaned near and asked, "What now? We didn't plan on a storm."

"It's always something, but this may work in our favor. As long as it storms, the Riddlings won't be leaving anytime soon. Laura and Lucy are out of the way, let's go down the back stairs to the kitchen and see what's happening downstairs."

"How do you know there's a back stairs?"

"I've been here before...when I picked up the trunk. It was in Betty Sue's bedroom, down the hall and to the left." She pointed in the general direction.

"Okay. You lead the way. Wait a minute." Abby Gayle quickly tiptoed to the bedroom door and gently turned the knob.

Returning, she said, "Laura is in bed with the cover over her head, and Lucy is resting in the chair with her eyes closed. It is getting late; both must be exhausted."

Jix started down the hallway to the stairs. "By the way, Sopakco is in the kitchen. It would not be wise to startle him; he carries a gun."

"I don't think he likes either of us. It's best we don't give him an excuse to shoot," Abby Gayle noted.

164

⚊

Meanwhile, Richard and Que had bolted through pelting rain to make their way to the detached garage where the whole house generator was kept. Richard had remarked that due to the history of storms in the area, whole house generators were common and had suggested they check the reset on the generator. If a power interruption lasted longer than a few minutes, the generator should activate automatically.

Bobby and Bethany sat on opposite ends of the couch. Que had hesitated to leave her alone with her nemesis but conceded when he remembered Sopakco was monitoring the den from the kitchen. Detectives Bird and Martino also lurked in the shadows...somewhere.

Chapter Thirty-One

The moment had arrived.

They were alone.

Lucy and Laura were upstairs, Richard and Que were in the garage, and Jix and Abby Gayle had arrived in the kitchen without a single shot fired even though Sopakco was somewhat less than thrilled to see the ladies.

Bethany waited for Bobby to make the first move.

The muted television flickered. Weatherman Tracey had shed his jacket and tie as he continued to pace with an air of urgency in front of a map splashed with flashing splotches of color.

She sat with her hands folded in her lap until he finally spoke.

"Pardon me, Barbara, but would I be mistaken if I said your name is not Barbara but Bethany?" He spoke louder than one would normally carry on a conversation to be heard over the unrelenting storm.

She inhaled deeply, raised her chin, and looked him squarely in the eye.

Calmly, she answered, "No. You would not be mistaken." There was no backing down now, so matter-of-factly, she stated, "I'm not running from you any longer, Bobby. I should have confronted you long ago."

A glimmer of his soft spot for her escaped his hardened gaze. "I've longed to tell you I mean you no harm. The two of us have a complicated history. Wouldn't you agree?"

"Bobby, I saw you drown Roselyn. Both Amelia and I knew she was pregnant. Remember the day I walked in on the two of you embracing? I knew then you were taking advantage of her. That was when I confronted Roselyn, and she told me everything. I also know on the day of the picnic, she told you that you were the father of her baby."

He chuckled. "I don't know what you are talking about. Regardless of anything you say, it is my word against yours. Always has been." He leisurely stretched his arm across the back of the sofa.

"Bobby, I saw you hold her under the water. You drowned her, and I saw you!" A brief wave of dizziness struck as she relived witnessing her friend fight to stay alive.

A hateful smirk swept across his face. "You think you know everything! And, what if you don't? What if I was trying to help her? What if Laura overheard when Roselyn told me she was pregnant, and what if she added an overdose of pills to Roselyn's drink? What if when the boat overturned, Roselyn was too drugged to save herself, and I was trying to help her? Also consider your predicament; you were on the brink of drowning at the time, therefore, reasonable grounds to question the certainty of what you think you witnessed."

"I know what I saw. You put forth no effort to help her, and you know it! Did Laura know you had gotten *another* young girl pregnant? Did Laura drug Roselyn, or is she once more your scapegoat? I don't believe you, Bobby! I don't believe anything you say!"

"Nobody cares! It doesn't matter what you believe or think or say. A jury would laugh should we ever go to trial...and that, by the way, I would not recommend. Sweetheart, it is my word against yours. There is no way anyone will believe you! Never!" As if he'd flipped a switch, his tone softened, "I've wanted to talk to you for so long. To explain. You know you'll always have a special place in my heart." He reached to hold her hand.

She pulled away.

Repulsed by the man she now faced, she was convinced Bobby Riddling would lie when the truth would do. At first, when he'd said she was special to him, she'd believed him. At the time, she'd been little more than a child.

At last, this man who had imprisoned her had with his manipulative rhetoric unknowingly set her free. Clearly, this man exploited anyone he could use to satisfy his purpose. Here was a man who lived a double life: sometimes a gentle man, a businessman, a charming, smooth-talker—other times a predator of innocents, a liar, and a vindictive, ruthless man.

She saw him as she'd never truthfully seen him before. The prison door to her tortured soul had swung open wide, releasing half a lifetime of pent up confusion, fear, and adversity. Words freely spilled from her mouth.

"And Amelia? Let's talk about Amelia," she said. "Was she blackmailing you? Threatening to tell what you had done to young girls? Did she threaten to reveal your family secrets?"

He hadn't seen that coming. "There is no proof of blackmail," Bobby sputtered. He folded his arms in defiance.

She continued, "Should her bank records show large deposits at regular intervals, will your bank records show matching withdrawals?" Surprise in his eyes empowered her.

"If anyone checks, they will find payments were made from Laura's checking account, certainly not from mine. Give me more credit than that," he sniggered. "Any checks Amelia may have received will have Laura's signature on them." A warmth rushed to his neck and cheeks as his heart rate increased.

"Come on, Bobby. You think I believe Laura would pay Amelia off to keep quiet about Paula?" she chortled. "You've taken me for a fool in the past, but I'm all grown up now. I'm not a scared little girl you can threaten and deceive. Amelia would never blackmail her sister. She loved Laura, and she had promised to keep Laura's secret. But she would blackmail you. She despised you, and if Laura signed checks made out to Amelia, it would be because Laura thought she was giving, not paying, the money to help her sister."

Bobby grinned. "Well, well, it's apparent you aren't as naïve as you once were. By the way, you were incredibly easy to talk into anything. These little innocents are stupidly vulnerable and starved for attention. I'm amused at how easily they submit. Some men like the thrill of the hunt. I like the naivety of the young," he sneered.

If he had twisted a knife in her chest, it could not have been more painful. Bethany, more determined than ever to bring him down, lifted her chin, tightened her eyes, and maintained a steady gaze of contempt.

He continued, "As for the payoffs, that is exactly the way it happened. Unknowingly, Laura paid her. There is nothing to tie me to a blackmail scheme. Nothing at all! And if Laura were convicted of anything, she'll be declared incompetent to stand trial. Easy-peasy, little Miss Know It All," he scoffed.

"So, you killed Amelia to keep her from telling your family secret and to end a blackmail scheme."

A subtle shift of command had occurred. As a sense of power and confidence swelled, she folded her arms, gesturing a barrier of strength. She had pushed him to the brink of confessing.

A creeping awareness of mounting inability to control his responses left Riddling shaken. "No! Bees killed her. She had a deadly reaction to bee stings." Anger had seeped past his intended boundaries fueling the loss of self-control.

She egged him on.

"Amelia always knew the truth, and you know what I am talking about. She kept your secret for decades. Why did she start blackmailing you after all these years? How did she lure her to the gazebo?"

"Not that it is any of your business, but they had accrued a lot of debt. Her husband gambles. As far as luring her, a few phone calls, a little sweet talk, and she willingly agreed to meet. In case you've forgotten, I have a way with women. Oops! I neglected to tell her I'd brought along a few angry bees. It doesn't take many; one bee can kill when the venom is deadly to its victim."

171

She breathed a sigh of relief. Hidden recorders had captured his confession. Detectives Bird and Martino had heard him confess.

"Just one more question. You can certainly afford to pay. Why kill her? She was your wife's sister! You really are a heartless rat, Bobby! You took Amelia's life; you have robbed me of my life. You are a shameless, pathetic womanizer who preyed, and more than likely still preys, on young women! You're a selfish, despicable rat!"

Bethany's rampage was the last straw. An avalanche of anger and indignation swept away any shred of self-control Bobby sought to hang on to.

Bethany unfolded her arms and scooted forward with her feet planted firmly on the floor the instant she sensed the dynamics in the room had shifted once again.

She had crossed a line, and the man she faced had become uncontrollably enraged.

He lashed out. "Of all the nerve! The little hellion wanted more money! Nobody backs me into a corner and lives to tell it!" He grabbed her wrist. "Including you! You know too much, and that will never do. You should have continued to run, my dear Bethany. Maybe you aren't smarter after all!"

He jerked her to her feet and spun her around. Clamping his hand over her mouth, he twisted her arm behind her back until she winced in pain.

"Out the front door! Don't make a sound, or I'll snap your neck like a dry twig," he growled, and pushed her toward the foyer.

Instantly, Sopakco, weapon drawn, struck the kitchen door, slinging it open so violently it banged against the wall. He rushed in with a loud command to let her go.

Jix and Abby Gayle huddled in the doorway.

Detective Bird burst into the room. Detective Martino rushed in from the opposite direction—the mad man caught in the sights of their weapons.

Detective Bird shouted, "Bethany, step away from him!"

With a double-handed grip on a revolver extended at arm's length, she motioned with the barrel for Bethany to move away without hesitation.

"Riddling, I've got a clear shot to your head. If I miss, and I won't, Martino or Sopakco will take you out. Don't be stupid! Let her go! Bethany, walk toward the kitchen!" she shouted. "Now!"

Bobby dropped his hands. Bethany cradled her aching arm and took a step forward.

Suddenly, as blistering as a dose of heavenly retribution, a blast of thunder rocked the house!

The women screamed.

Panic-stricken, Lucy herded Laura down the stairs, dodging frantic dogs, as tens of thousands of amperes surged along a lightning channel.

With the deadliness and speed of a striking serpent, a deafening boom like a string of high explosives detonating at once, left no doubt that a wicked bolt of lightning had struck its target.

And then, in one huge, hungry gulp, darkness instantly swallowed the house and all those inside.

Chapter Thirty-Two

"So, let me get this straight," said sleep deprived, tousle-haired, Bill Haynes, propped upright with pillows stacked against the headboard. A hyped-up, soaking wet wife had awakened him from a sound sleep at two in the morning with a tale to rival an Agatha Christie mystery.

"Richard's malfunctioning generator functioned when Richard and Que pushed the reset button," he sought affirmation of her last statement.

"Right." Jix tied her robe at the waist and unfurled a towel turban from her freshly shampooed head. The rain-soaked clothes she'd worn to Ramone's were piled on the bathroom floor beside her new, now ruined, suede pumps from Penney's spring shoe sale.

She resumed her tale through the opened bathroom door, "They'd returned from the garage when the power went off. It should have come on again when the generator kicked in automatically, but it didn't, not until Richard and Que went back to the garage and pressed the reset button."

"And during the brief blackout, Bobby fled out the front door with Bethany." Bill took a shot at moving this story along.

"Correct. But the generator at Laura's house across the street came on when the electricity went off, so there was light from Richard's porch. But it didn't matter. Bethany would have tripped him whether there was light or not. She is one tough cookie! I want to be like her when I grow up." She grinned when a replay of Bobby Riddling spread eagle on the sidewalk came to mind.

"And I assume there was light from the fire at the house next door."

"Right again. Lightning struck...ran in through the wiring and blew the outlets all to hell. Set the whole place on fire. Within minutes, the fire truck arrived, making enough noise to wake the dead with the siren wailing like a banshee." As an afterthought, she added, "Although lightning striking the largest house in the neighborhood may have done more to wake the neighborhood than the siren. Up and down the street, people stood in the rain hoping the firemen, and the downpour, would save the house. I'm telling you, Bill, it was like a three-ring circus. I would not have been surprised a bit to see a car full of clowns drive up."

"Dear Lord," he moaned. Only his wife could see such a harrowing event as being comparable to a Ringling Brothers Barnum & Bailey Circus. He cut her some slack when he considered the wee, early hours of the morning and then factored in an ample production of adrenaline from hours of energy depleting excitement. The woman was running on fumes.

176

Jix walked barefoot across the carpet, pulled out the stool to her dressing table, and sat down. She blinked at the image in the mirror. Puffy eyelids and purple circles under her eyes were reminders she had been up half the night and on pins and needles all day.

She talked on, "Detective Bird and her cohorts descended on Bobby and snatched his sorry rear end out of a puddle. He'd fallen down the porch steps and broken his nose when Bethany tripped him. He'd bitten his lip and said his tooth was chipped. One of the firemen administered first aid once they'd gotten him back inside Richard's house. His nose bled while they read him his rights."

"How did Laura take all this?" He stifled a yawn.

"Not very well. She'd been beside herself since she'd first heard of storm warnings. She fretted until she drove herself into a mental stupor. She's not well, Bill. She's really not well at all."

"I suspected as much. So how will she handle her husband going to jail?"

"Lucy called Laura's doctor even though it was the middle of the night. Apparently, he has treated her for a number of years. He advised they take her to the hospital at Hillcrest where she has been treated before. Richard and Lucy admitted her, and Lucy may have stayed the night. I'm not sure. I need to check on her in the morning...both Laura and Lucy."

"Well, all's well that ends well." He closed his eyes. At last they could get some sleep.

"Oh, it didn't end there," she said, laying the hairbrush on the dresser.

His eyes popped open. Dear God. Was there no rest for the weary?

She pumped lotion from a bottle and rubbed it on her arms. "Before they left to take Laura, Bethany dropped a bombshell...and in the presence of Bobby and Laura. We were all there—everybody heard."

"I'm afraid to ask what she said." He slid to a supine position and adjusted the pillows.

"Seems Bobby is not the only liar in this postulated sequence of events. Bethany explained she wanted closure, complete closure. To accomplish total transparency, she had to reveal she had lied about Amelia having a child with Bobby Riddling. She stunned everyone in the room, Laura and Bobby being the exception. They already knew. Amelia is not Paula's biological mother...Bethany is."

"What? Riddling and Bethany!" He was wide-awake once more.

"I'm telling you what she said. Bobby Riddling coerced her into an inappropriate relationship the year before she graduated high school when she was seventeen. She was dating Que, but she says Bobby molested her for quite some time. She tried to tell Laura, but Laura wouldn't listen. She became aggressive toward Bethany, treated her horribly."

"Well, if that don't beat all," he shook his head in dismay.

Jix kept talking, "Bethany and Amelia went away for a year. Amelia went with Bethany as a friend helping a friend in need. It sounds like they were closer than the twins were; however, Lucy and Laura do not fit into a typical twin mold. While the girls were away, Bobby and Laura also moved, on the pretext Bobby was going to school. They played out this elaborate scheme, convincing everyone Laura had had a baby. Both Bobby's and

Bethany's reputations were saved, and the baby had a home."

"How could Lucy not know about this? Or did she?"

"No, she didn't know. Only Amelia knew, and that is what she used to blackmail Bobby. She threatened to tell everyone that Bethany gave birth to Paula. Bill, this is the weirdest family I've ever known when it comes to keeping secrets. Our lives are like an open book compared to theirs. I shudder to think what else they may be hiding."

"What about Paula's sister? Is she Laura's child? Is she Bobby's child?

Jix didn't want to go there. "Lord only knows."

She remembered a detail as to why the trunk had come their way. "Bethany had specified upon Amelia's death the trunk should go to Paula. When Bethany learned Amelia had died, she was anxious to know if her wish had been carried out. If I've understood correctly, she saw the trunk loaded on a delivery truck and followed it here. That's how she found Paula, Laura, and Lucy."

"She was staking out Amelia's house?"

"Sounds like it."

Bill wondered, "I've been thinking about a time lapse. When did Bethany write the coded message in the diary? It would have had to have been after the drowning. If she and Que left town immediately, when did she record the message?"

"I wondered that too. From what I've been able to piece together, immediately after the drowning, Bethany went to her mother's house. She penned the words in green ink and coded the message. Her mother took the diary to Amelia later. She and Amelia may have met at some point...I'm not sure. But she told Amelia to get the trunk from her mother and protect it. Details are a bit fuzzy."

"How did Laura react when Bethany divulged the Riddling family secret? And Que? What about him? Did he know Bethany had had Bobby's child?" Bill asked.

"As for Laura, she had pretty well checked in to wherever she goes when she can't cope with reality. I'm not certain she understood anything anyone said. Richard and Lucy were, as to be expected, in shock. As for Que, I think Bethany's confession answered more than one question for him, such as why she is so driven and basically unhappy. I think the person she has really been running away from all these years is herself. Que loves Bethany, and she loves him; they'll be alright."

"Did Bobby deny it?"

"He refused to say anything until his lawyer was present, and he wanted to see a doctor. On top of everything else, Detective Bird is going to charge him with kidnapping. Although he didn't get far with Bethany, he took her against her will."

"Paula is coming home to a few surprises, isn't she? She may need another vacation after she finds out her mother is not her mother, and her aunts are not her aunts, and her father is a murderous playboy," he said.

"I know. And the five girls...they have a new grandmother. This is like a soap opera."

"I may call Richard and see if he needs to vent—man to man, you know. Not that I want to get involved, but I can listen if he wants a brother to talk to."

Jix pondered the brother offer. It was so unlike Bill to risk involvement in anyone's "business." *Stay out of it* was his mantra.

Final dabs of night cream in the right places, and she was ready for bed. She remembered the wet clothes in the bathroom. They would still be there in the morning. She would deal with them then.

"Bethany wants to go with Abby Gayle and me when we deliver the trunk," she said. "It belonged to her grandmother, and she wants Paula to know the history. And she wants her daughter to know her biological mother. I can only imagine the loneliness and frustration Bethany has endured most of her life. I trust the future will be brighter for her and Que."

"I hope so, and I hope she realizes Que is a hellavu man. He seems to have honored the 'or worse' part of his marriage vows beyond the call of duty."

"She does. She adores him; he's a very decent man. I find him pretty easy to like…and it seems she finds him easy to love."

Fumbling for the chain on the bedside lamp, she turned off the light and climbed into bed, snuggling close to her husband in a loose spoon position.

He felt her warmth. Her damp hair smelled like strawberries; he closed his eyes and inhaled the fragrance. Within minutes, her breathing was steady and deep.

"Does this mean Bobby won't be playing golf tomorrow?"

The only response was a rhythmic stream of barely audible snores coming from the love of his life.

Chapter Thirty-Three

The black sedan that had once come close to being a lethal weapon rolled onto Abby Gayle's driveway and stopped behind Jix's truck. Securely bungeed to the truck bed, Betty Sue Manikin's graduation gift had been restored to its former grandeur, and then some. The trunk was structurally sound because it had been kept inside and taken care of for the past one hundred years. Polished metal, refinished wood, a new smell, a new look, a fresh decorative design inside, and Bethany's trunk had become a reclaimed jewel to be treasured by generations to come.

The garage door was up, and Jix was sweeping the floor when Bethany got out of the car and walked toward her.

"Come in," Abby Gayle came from inside and stood beside Jix. They had not seen Bethany since the night of her award-winning performance at Richard's.

Under her breath, Jix commented, "A bit different approach than the last time she came into your garage."

"SSShhh. And thankfully so."

The person given a new lease on life greeted Jix and Abby Gayle with a warm radiance. The new Bethany was pretty. The frightened woman they'd first met, posing as a man, had taken leave, and the business of catching a killer had drawn the women into a solid sisterhood of unity and loyalty.

Following a round of hugs, Jix offered to show Bethany her restored trunk, but she chose to wait for the reveal when Paula and Betty Sue were present. In the den, Abby Gayle and Jix had once again unpacked the cardboard box and displayed the trunk contents on a card table. Abby Gayle had checked her list to be sure they'd not overlooked anything.

Rediscovering her treasures rippled a deep-seated pool of tenderness. Amelia had promised her dear friend she would keep her belongings safe until she returned, and Amelia had done so. She had remained a loving and loyal friend to the end.

Embracing her emotions, Bethany lingered over each item. Her fingertips caressed the sheet music as she told how she had taken piano lessons from Miss Hilda who, back then, also played the organ at the Methodist Church.

Every item had a story, and every story came with an emotional tug. Three generations of women in Bethany's family had treasured the hand-carved marble, cameo broaches. She closed her eyes and fingered an oval cameo of Madonna and Child on a black background, summoning a time-faded recollection of the broach pinned to Grandmother's Sunday dress.

The strand of pearls, a birthstone for June babies, had been a gift from her mother when she'd turned sixteen.

184

Jix asked, "Tell us about your mother. Do you know where she is?"

"Oh yes, she lives with my older sister Victoria and her family." She thought for a second, then added, "Vickie's children are grown now. I called Mother from time to time at first, but I suspected Bobby was having her watched. I suppose he thought I might go to see her, so I stopped calling. At Christmas and on her birthday, I would phone and ask for someone...a name I'd made up. Mother would say I had the wrong number. It was a way of letting her know I was alive. Bobby visited her once or twice and asked if she knew how he could contact me. I was both saddened and encouraged by the sound of her voice every time I called."

Jix thought of her own mother whom she saw every day, and she understood Bethany's heartache.

Abby Gayle led the way to the kitchen. "We'll pack these things in a smaller box for you to take with you. Then we'll deliver the trunk to Paula. I made a chocolate cake with strawberry frosting. Let's have a slice, sit, and relax for a while, and you can tell us what has transpired in the past week." A grin spread on Bethany's lips. She knew she was in the South where cake was the common denominator for most occasions.

Late afternoon sun streamed through the upper panes of a window with café curtains covering the lower half. Turned down low, Milli Vanilli sang *Blame It On The Rain* over a small radio sitting next to a stack of cookbooks on top of the refrigerator. The aroma of freshly baked cake perfumed the air.

When everyone was seated and the baker had been lavished with compliments for a tasty cake, Jix said to

Bethany, "Paula has been back for several days. How did your meeting with her go?"

"Well, first of all, let me say Richard Manikin is a wonderful man. Thanks to him, who'd explained everything that has happened in her absence, she chose to meet with me. I left it up to Paula. Que and I had discussed and agreed we would move on if she did not want to see me. All I ever had of my baby was a lock of hair Amelia had cut when she babysat. For the first two or three years, Amelia would leave things in our secret place, and I would check every year or so. Que and I would sneak into town at night, check the hiding place, and leave before anyone saw us," she explained. "Paula is debating about how to tell her girls Laura raised her but is not her birth mother."

Abby Gayle commented as she refilled cups. "She's a courageous woman. Paula has my admiration. It must surely have been a shock finding out Laura is not her biological mother—not to mention the news about her father. Speaking of Laura, how is she?"

"Richard tells me she won't be coming home any time soon. Her doctor recommends long-term, institutional care. Lucy says she knew it would come to this sooner or later. They never talked about Laura being mentally and developmentally impaired as a result of mild oxygen deprivation at birth. Actually, I don't think much was known about the condition when she was born. It is no wonder she grew up believing if a matter is ignored, it ceases to exist." Bethany paused reflectively. "I've wondered if Bobby married her to take advantage of her limitations. From the beginning, she catered to his every whim in her child-like way. She defended him by turning

186

a blind eye to things that would have been obvious to most wives."

"And perhaps he married her because he loved her." Jix chased a crumb before pushing her plate aside. "I've talked to Richard several times since that stormy night. He tells me he plans to do something with Laura's house, sell it or rent it. Is there a possibility you and Que may be interested?"

"We've talked about it. A lot depends on whether Paula wants me as a neighbor. I've suddenly appeared from nowhere. Moving into Laura's house may be too much. I'll respect Paula's wishes. Wherever we move, moving is a must. We've enjoyed the log house on the crest, and it has been a godsend in time of need, but it is sooooo remote. I can only imagine what getting up the mountain in the winter would be like." She sipped her coffee that had cooled to lukewarm. "Believe it or not, I miss Sopakco. Beneath his hard exterior is a sweet guy." Since he was no longer her shadow, she'd found it easier to see him as less annoying.

They laughed hysterically when Jix told how aggravated the old cop with bunions had been with her and Abby Gayle from the moment he'd cracked open the door at the Doe Ridge house. "He was suspicious of us from the start. We feared he'd shoot us if we surprised him when we crept downstairs to Richard's kitchen."

Abby Gayle spoke up, "Back to Laura's house. Will it come with two black cats? Heed a word of advice; if you rent or buy, don't include the furniture. It's archaic. And ugly. And for Pete's sake, open up the windows. Take down those dreadful drapes."

Jix hesitated to criticize another's taste in interior design, but she could not resist adding, "The wallpaper. I trust you will be replacing the wallpaper."

How good it was to laugh with friends. Bethany had to pinch herself as a reminder this wasn't a dream even though she had never dreamed of such joy that included new friends. This would take getting used to.

She said with heartfelt admiration, "Thanks again, you two. Words are inadequate to express my appreciation for all you've done…and for how you've opened your homes and your hearts to us." Her eyes misted. "I don't know if you've heard, but Que is working full time for Richard; this is his third day on the new job. We at least have a steady income for the first time in a while. Keep your fingers crossed; I've applied for a teller's position at the bank. And I'm going to let my hair grow…I'm looking forward to shoulder length hair again." She tousled her cropped cut.

"Que's such a nice guy; he'll be a successful salesman. I'd buy a car from him," Jix said.

"Me too," Abby Gayle added, "and I may. I've been thinking of trading my car."

"I'll tell him to check with you. Richard told me they are taking Bobby back to Mississippi to stand trial for Amelia's murder. I'm not certain if they will charge him with Roselyn's death at this time or perhaps later. It will be his word against mine unless more evidence is discovered as they investigate," Bethany blinked back tears. She'd not properly grieved her dear friend's passing. She and her husband would visit Amelia's gravesite in the near future.

Jix stacked the plates and cups. Abby Gayle placed the glass dome over the cake and left it on the countertop.

Thoughtfully, Bethany stated, "I don't want to replace Laura. She is the mother Paula knows, the grandmother the children know. I hope she will be part of their lives to whatever extent she is able. I don't want to mother Paula; I want to be her friend. I've told her these things."

Jix expressed her support. "You two will work it out. She didn't know any of this until she came home. I'm sure it has been a lot to digest. It has been a lot for us to digest."

Abby Gayle pushed her chair back under the table. "Are you ready to go? Bethany, one more thing; I know you moved a lot, but did you ever stay in one place for long?"

"The longest was when we were out West. We lived in Denver for almost five years. We worked wherever we could find work. We moved when I felt threatened," Bethany said. She and Jix scooted their chairs away from the table. Jix put a few pieces of silverware in the dishwasher.

"In what way?" Abby Gayle asked.

Bethany dropped her head, "The truth is, now this is over and so much has come to light, I realize I had become paranoid. I didn't trust anyone but Que. And honestly, a few times, I doubted him. You have given me the courage to trust again. I am thinking clearer now than I have in years. Finally, I have closure. Everything is out in the open; Bobby is being held accountable for what he has done, and I can face that I've lived a lie. I've lied to my husband and to myself."

Bethany reached for a napkin she'd folded and left on the table, "If it weren't for my husband, I think I would have lost my mind. He often told me I was overreacting, but I wouldn't listen. If I thought we were in danger and wanted to relocate, Que was supportive. Now that I can think sensibly, I know I was probably as big a threat to myself as Bobby Riddling ever was. I should have stood up to him years ago. If I could turn back time...."

Jix reached for her hand. "We would all do certain things differently if the opportunity were available. All that matters is you and your husband can find the happiness you deserve. You have no power to change the past, but the future will be as bright as you make it." She reassured her with a gentle pat on the shoulder. "We need to go. Paula is expecting us."

Bethany reminded them, "Yes, we do. Let's not forget to put the trunk contents in my car. As I've said, Betty Sue and the other girls don't know about me. I'll share with them that Amelia and I were friends and tell them we shared the trunk. I'm quite excited to meet the girls and tell them about Amelia."

Jix didn't say so, but she was excited for Bethany to meet Diana, the third oldest daughter, who happened to be the spitting image of her grandmother.

The phone rang. Abby Gayle conversed briefly and then reported to the others; Richard and Que were on the way, and they should wait for them.

To pass the time, they packed the trunk items in a smaller box and loaded it in Bethany's car. Jix kept her opinions to herself, but she hoped soon the car salesman husband could swing a deal for his wife to drive a newer car. The sedan was showing its age.

The women stood in the garage talking while they waited for the men to arrive.

"There comes Richard," Abby Gayle spotted his car approaching. They waved, and he tooted the horn. The ladies could see Que sitting in the front seat. There appeared to be passengers in the backseat.

Richard swung wide and parked beside Bethany's car.

He and Que got out as the girls met them. Richard reached behind him and opened the back door. Que opened the other.

Out stepped Bethany's mother.

And out stepped Victoria.

THE END

If you've appreciated this book, would you mind taking the time to leave an online review? Go to www.SaraMcFerrin.com for links to online sellers.

Thank you!